The Domain of Dreams

Written by Derek McMillan

Edited by Angela McMillan

Introduction

Who reads introductions? Personally, I always prefer to get into the story or stories without any preamble. This is a collection of short stories based on #themirrorofeternity. It is the fifth book in the series – how time flies when you are enjoying yourself – details of the other four books are to be found at the end of this volume.

I am a writer from Durrington-on-Sea in West Sussex. My wife is Angela McMillan who edits my work. We are both former teachers.

I enjoy writing Science Fiction because of the free range it gives to the imagination. One of the first Sci Fi novels I read was "Rip Foster rides the Grey Planet" I read it under the blankets with the aid of a torch. I was supposed to be asleep. Even as a youngster I could tell some of the things in the book were just plain daft but it was not just the book itself which inspired me. It was also the humour and the vast possibilities which Sci Fi offered for story telling.

The #mirrorofeternity series has given me the freedom to look at serious historical events (past, present and future) and explore the light and dark sides of them.

What is the Mirror of Eternity? I first came across the idea in a philosophy text book which referred to the mirror of eternity as a reference point for our earthly pre-occupations. It may seem very important to us whether the government moves to the right or the left, whether we are wearing the right socks or whether West Ham do well this season. In the mirror of eternity these things may be less important than we think.

Science tells us that we cannot travel in time the way H G Wells envisaged. It would create too many paradoxes. Has this stopped Sci-Fi writers experimenting with the idea of time travel? Of course not. In the mind we can go to any place or any time. The Mirror of Eternity program, written by Dr Xavier Hollands and Dr Tilly Hollands is not scientific. It is the place where dreams and reality meet.

The other strand to the #mirrorofeternity is the ancient concept of astral projection. This has a long and honourable tradition in Eastern and Western thought. It also has untold possibilities for fun.

The stories in this volume are:

The Dreamscape – Tilly and Xavier explore the possibilities which astral projection present to them. In your dreams you have as much strength as you can imagine. With practice and discipline you can imagine quite a lot.

The Death of Xavier's Parents – people have asked about this after enigmatic comments in two of the #mirrorofeternity books. Here the whole story is unfolded.

If Xavier ruled the world – Just a bit of fun after the rather heavy implications of the previous story.

Hospital Prison – People in intensive care are not really aware of their surroundings. They are asked by staff every single time they see them, "Do you know where you are?" One of the most common illusions people in this situation have is that they are in prison. This was written shortly after I escaped from hospital. I will say here and now that the way I was treated by the nursing and nursing auxiliary staff was exemplary. It is nevertheless the case that most of the

4

patients I encountered in hospital were very keen to get out of there.

Something in the Air, Grosvenor Square – Thunderclap Newman's "Something in the Air" came out in 1969. The first anti-war demonstrations in Grosvenor Square were in 1968. The dirty tricks used against the anti-war movement by the police only came to light more recently when a number of under-cover cops were exposed.

Ouija – The Ouija board has always fascinated people. In the past a pack of Lexicon cards and a glass served the same purpose and this little bit of black magic became a family game. It has a sinister side though. Ask Tiberius.

The Dictator and the Clairvoyant – There were rumours in London that Winston Churchill consulted black magicians and astrologers for a hint of what Hitler was thinking. Dennis Wheatley worked for him at the time and his book, "They used dark forces" is a fictional account of Nazi links with Satanism.

The Future – the Mirror of Eternity program is a way to look into the past but it could also be used to look into the future despite the dangers which this would present. What if you created a parallel universe and could not get back to this one? Would you even know this is what you have done or would the universe seem just the same to you? Or is this just a load of mumbo jumbo?

The Robinson Report – while I was in hospital I had a recurring dream and this story is an example of making use of a dream for a story. The dream was darker than the story.

The Seeds of Time – as well as being a quote from Macbeth, this is also the title of a John Wyndham short story collection which I enjoyed as a youngster. It is another example of using the Mirror of Eternity to look into the future.. The sardonic voice of Wolf-Dietrich von Raitenau is heard in this story too.

Visit to Tellus – Xavier couldn't resist visiting a planet where the historians studied 'Xavierology' and the Mirror of Eternity was in use on a wide scale.

The Impossible Co-ordinates – It is assumed that human life can only exist on earth-like planets within the "Goldilocks zone" - not too hot not too cold. It ain't necessarily so.

Tellurian – would an attempt to foil the saving of the human race lead to the creation of a parallel universe where there were no humans? Or is that a load of mumbo-jumbo too?

Xavier is missing – many people have wanted to kill Xavier but has somebody finally succeeded?

The Ghost of Whitebeam Woods – Whitebeam Woods is a real place. This is a story based on our experiences and imagination.

Defending Academics Against Libel – To finish off, a lighthearted story about libel in the academic world.

I hope you enjoy these stories.

Derek McMillan

The Dreamscape

They were in a secure room which could only be accessed by an app on Xavier or Tilly's phone and only then by someone who knew the password. Five candles burnt at the vertices of the pentacle and there was a circle of holy water around it. Tilly and Xavier lay naked in the pentacle itself and looked up at the ceiling. The ceiling was a large screen which briefly displayed the "Mirror of Eternity" logo.

They both felt the aches and tensions of the day slipping away from them as they projected themselves into the dreamscape.

They were walking down a straight path in the woods. It was so straight because it had once been a railway track. The sunlight (it was always summer here) was filtered through the leaves of the trees.

In time they reached a particular pile of railway sleepers and here they left all the worries of everyday life behind to be called for on their return. The sleepers were on the left of the path. On the right was a stile. They climbed over the stile and walked hand in hand along a footpath through a field which was a riot of colour as wild flowers seemed to vie with each other for their attention. They had no sense of smell in the dreamscape but they still sought to catch the scent of the flowers.

They tarried a while by a waterfall in a woodland glade. Apart from the way they had come there were three other paths leading from the glade.

At length they stood up. Xavier easily tossed the rock they had been sitting on to Tilly who as easily caught it. Their strength in the dreamscape was as much as their imagination could make it. Their ability to read minds needed practice however. That was the way that they justified these frequent visits to the dreamscape to themselves.

They agreed to venture down the leftmost path. Tilly had adopted the plain clothing of Sister Lam and Xavier was trying to look like a lay brother of the Order of St Katherine.

They came to a well where a solitary woman was drawing water. Xavier detected a very strong message that Eva had a distrust of men. He let sister Lam do the talking and he made use of one of the conjuring tricks Wolf-Dietrich had passed on to him. He could produce a book of his choice from thin air. He chose to produce it from the folds of his habit which seemed more seemly.

In this case it was "*The Consolations of Philosophy*" by Boetheus as amended by Xavier Hollands. He tucked in to the chapter on parallel universes. He could also hear the conversation of Sister Lam and Eva as well as reading a fair amount of their thought.

Eva, it seemed, was not married to the smith in the local village but he still made her fetch and carry and cook and have sex with him when he so desired. He liked it but wouldn't put a ring on it.

"What does the priest think about that?"

"What is a priest?"

"We only know one priest," was Sister Lam's thought, directed at Xavier. She referred to the August Prince-Archbishop of Salzburg, Wolf-Dietrich von Raitenau. Although he was not a Prince or an Archbishop in this reality he was a priest. The phrase 'once a priest always a priest' is more true than you may know.

"Do you think Wolf-Dietrich goes to every village without a priest to conduct weddings?" asked Xavier mildly

"Well it would depend if he was in a good mood." Sister

10

Lam insisted, adding, "There is something distinctly odd about this village and the local city which they only refer to as 'The Ship.'"

Xavier walked off into the forest and vanished as soon as he was out of Eva's sight.

The journey from the bright sunlight to the gloom of St Sebastian's Churchyard in ancient Salzburg was achieved in the blink of an eye. Xavier found himself looking at the monument to bad taste which was the mausoleum of Wolf-Dietrich von Raitenau. Wolf-Dietrich himself was rather pointedly looking away from it.

He didn't need to explain his mission because Wolf-Dietrich could read his mind with ease. To say that Wolf-Dietrich was in a good mood would not be strictly true but he was amenable to the request of his young friend. He too thought "The Ship" was worthy of investigation and he did have a pastoral duty towards the smith and Eva.

The smith, whose name really was John, agreed to being baptised and married after Wolf-Dietrich put the fear of God into him or, more likely, put the fear of Wolf-Dietrich into him.

Wolf-Dietrich was overwhelmed by the number of villagers

who wanted to be baptised and married but his sense of duty compelled him to fulfil his priestly function.

Xavier translated the Rosary into the local language and then he and Sister Lam taught it to any of the villagers who were interested. In the event that was 25 in a village of 34 which was quite gratifying. Naturally the Rosary led on to all kinds of questions from the villagers but Xavier was one of those people who enjoy answering questions. In turn he asked his own questions.

"The local town (the word actually translated as 'big village") is know as 'The Ship' does anybody know why that is?" There was a silence at this and it was only John Smith who dared to speak up.

"Well there are only children's stories and old wives' tales about that. They do say as how a ship was wrecked and the survivors built the town. Funny sort of ship it must have been because there is no sea around these parts and many of the houses in the town were built of metal not timber. Nobody has ever heard tell of a ship built of metal. I mean it would sink to the bottom of the sea for a start."

"I know about it because once in a while somebody from The Ship will call on me for a bit of metal-work. In exchange there are one or two neat little tricks with metal-work which they have taught to me."

It seemed that apart from their commerce with the smith, the people of The Ship tended to keep themselves to themselves. Although it appeared they had a level of technology streets ahead of the villagers they had no great urge to share it.

"I am suspicious of this." was Xavier's thought.

"Because they must have their own metal-work facilities and no need of the smith's assistance." Wolf-Dietrich completed his thought for him.

"Perhaps," Sister Lam added, "they are seeking to recruit the locals who will be of most use to them."

"So do we wait for them to recruit John Smith, which could take a while, or do we make our own way to The Ship?" Xavier asked.

It gave Wolf-Dietrich a certain pleasure to say, "Their level of technology is ahead of yours, possibly by centuries. They may have mastered mind-reading which would place you at a disadvantage."

"On the other hand," Xavier said slowly, "It would be fascinating to see the workings of an advanced civilisation.

13

Disadvantage or no."

The journey to The Ship was rather longer than they had thought it would be. The area was heavily wooded and they had to make their own path through the trees and shrubs. They had a sample of Wolf-Dietrich's astro-navigation but they soon realised that "the stars were all wrong" or they were on another planet.

In the end they stood on a hill and saw it spread before them. The town actually glittered because of the number of metal buildings.

As they descended towards The Ship they all had the same experience. One minute they were walking towards the town, the next they were lying unconscious on the ground.

Xavier and Sister Lam opened their eyes at about the same time. They were lying in a brightly-lit chamber. They were held to their beds by wrist and ankle restraints. These they broke easily and stood up.

They heard a familiar voice. "Nothing in Heaven or Earth should be able to fell an astral projection like that." said Wolf-Dietrich, appearing out of thin air as was his disconcerting habit.

"I think," said Xavier, "that it must be a defence system

designed to keep the more curious members of the local peasantry at bay. It is a warning to us that the people of The Ship are hostile to outsiders and they have the power to render us unconscious."

"Can they kill us?" Sister Lam's question hung in the air for a long moment. None of them knew the answer to that.

"You will have noticed that this room has no door." Wolf-Dietrich said. In fact they hadn't but a swift look around the room confirmed the fact that it held two beds and nothing else. No means of entrance was apparent and the walls seemed seamless.

"You have spoken enough," said a voice. To Xavier and Sister Lam it seemed to speak in unaccented English. To Wolf-Dietrich it spoke in faultless Latin.

"You will explain your mission here. It is clear to us that you are not of this world. In fact you have let slip that you are astral projections. It is pointless to lie to us so you, I mean **you** Wolf-Dietrich, will tell us exactly what your mission and intentions are or none of you will leave this room alive."

Wolf-Dietrich mustered his dignity and power, which was considerable, and went into a rapid explanation in Latin which Xavier and Sister Lam could not keep pace with very easily. Their later translations show some of the flavour.

"We are unarmed. We have come on a mission of peace to bring comfort and hope to the poor peasants of this country. We are explorers and naturally we took an interest in The Ship, as this place is known locally. We have made no hostile moves or gestures towards you. You are right in thinking that we are astral projections..."

"The other two are different from you. They have physical form and you seem weak and formless."

"Nevertheless, we come in peace. Xavier and Sister Lam are indeed hard astral projections but they too have made no threatening moves against the town or its inhabitants."

"You, Xavier, what is your mission of peace?"

"I am here to assist Sister Lam and Father Wolf-Dietrich in bringing the message of Jesus Christ to the local people."

As Xavier had hoped this led off into a discussion about the nature of God. It was apparent that the people of The Ship had some knowledge of religion. Their interrogator, however, was one of those people who could see no world beyond the here and now. He also had a contempt for the local peasants. He thought of them as beings beneath his notice; a nuisance to be kept at bay.

16

"Yet you trade with the smiths." Sister Lam interjected. She was more than a little displeased at the male-dominated discussion.

"Ah. Sister Lam, I was coming to you. You have had sexual intercourse with Xavier and yet you claim to be a devotee of St Katherine in this reality."

"We are all devotees of St Katherine," she retorted.

She unconsciously folded her arms across her chest and put her feet a shoulder width apart. She would defend her devotion to St Katherine to the death.

Her mind was taken back to the Marian blue room where 'Doctor Katherine' (as she introduced herself) had taught her the ways of the dreamscape. Doctor Katherine had alternately amused and instructed her and taught her to look deeply into her own feelings. She adored the Saint but more than that she loved the woman. She could easily believe that St Katherine had converted the greatest thinkers of the pagan world to her Christianity. Those philosophers knew that they condemned themselves to martyrdom by converting. Yet still they became followers of Christ.

From the Diary of Wolf-Dietrich von Raitenau

While Sister Lam was confronting our interrogator with her devotion to St Katherine it seemed a good time to breach the door-less wall. I found myself in what I thought of as a steel corridor although I am no metallurgist and it was probably some other more exotic alloy. It was less brightly-lit than the room I had left but my eyes adjusted to the gloom and I was able to make my way.

I soon found our interrogator. He had obligingly left the door of his room open. A definitely human figure of about forty years of age sat at his ease in front of a console. He was drinking a sparkling blue drink and ridiculing Sister Lam.

I used a little conjuring trick to move the cursor on his screen to keep his microphone on so what my young friends heard was as follows.

"What are you doing? This is an act of aggression!"

"Do you mind if I sit down?"

"This is an attack on the integrity of The Ship!"

"Yet still you don't kill me. My name is Father Wolf-Dietrich and I forgive you for your hostility because you do not know what you are doing. It would be polite for the assassin to

18

give me his name."

Pause.

"Elliott"

"That is an English name and from the twenty first, twenty second century?"

"Twenty first."

"Good, Elliott now before we have a nice long chat I have one request. Let my people go."

Xavier and Sister Lam assure me that part of the wall simply de-materialised and they went into the corridor. Soon we were all together in the room. Elliott had to bring in another chair to accommodate us all. He offered us all some of the sparkling blue liquid which my young friends wisely declined. They would neither eat nor drink in the dreamscape.

Now that his empty threat to kill us had evaporated he was able to tell us his story. And what a story it was.

Eliott's Story

"Perilous to us all are the devices of an art deeper than we possess ourselves." You may have heard of the writer J R R

Tolkien and he never uttered a truer sentence.

I was born in 1999, long after Tolkien's "Lord of the Rings" was in the public domain. The book was often imitated but never surpassed. While I was studying politics at Cambridge I became acquainted with a Tolkien Society which taught Elvish to its members and had long readings from The Lord of the Rings and the Silmarillion which went on late into the night and required large amounts of beer and pizza to sustain them. In short I was living the life of a student and loving it.

There was an inner circle to the Tolkien society and I was eventually invited to join this secret group. I had to swear an oath in perfect High Elvish with a naked sword pointed at my Adam's apple. Then the blindfold was whipped off and I was offered a lager. It was all good fun. Or so I thought.

One night I was visited by two members of the inner circle. They waved aside my offer of drinks and intimated that I was to stick to water myself. I was mystified. They reminded me that I had sworn in High Elvish not to reveal the secrets of the inner circle to anyone *on pain of death.*

As if to make the point, one of them, Grant, produced a Luger. God alone knows where he got this relic. It sat on the occasional table like a threat. It had one purpose, to kill. And it was casually pointed in my direction.

"Politicians," he said with undisguised contempt, "always believe they can keep scientific secrets." I should mention that both Owen and Grant were scientists and thought politics was unscientific nonsense. Actually they had a point and in any case I make it a principle not to argue with a man with a gun.

"We know, though it is probable that the Science Minister has been kept in the dark about it, that there is a project codenamed 'Midgard' which makes use of technology which has been shared with a dissident group in the American military.

"The aim is to build a ship which will be able to cross the divide between parallel universes and take us to Middle Earth. It will be ten years before it nears completion."

"I have already been approached to do a hush-hush programming job with a very high price tag. Reading between the lines, the work can only be connected with Project Midgard. As a member of the inner circle it will be up to you to find a role in the Project and it will be our job to help you into it. Do you understand?"

21

He didn't have to put a pistol to my head. I had no career plans at that time and although I secretly thought Project Midgard would come to nothing I was quite happy to take the Government's money for a few years. Who knows, it could have led to a proper job in the Ministry of Agriculture. It didn't.

I started out as an Executive Officer in the Ministry of Science. With the aid of another member of the Inner Circle I was transferred to the section dealing with Project Midgard. I had to turn down one or two chances of promotion to stay in that department and my section head thought my behaviour was eccentric. That is until he was replaced with another member of the Inner Circle.

Five members of the Inner Circle had taken RAF scholarships and were able to train as pilots. Three of them failed the reaction times test but were able to get other jobs aboard The Ship. A decision was taken at the highest level that the crew of the good ship Midgard would consist largely of experts on Midgard. I am prepared to bet a sizeable sum that it was the only job in the British military where a knowledge of Elvish was regarded as an advantage.

It turned out that Grant and Owen were right. Even up to the launch the Science Minister was told that the enormous expenditure on Midgard was essential to the War against Terror and he (one of them was actually a she) had to be content with that.

We assembled on a chilly October morning. Our training regime had gone on in secret for three months. It was as harsh as the Inner Circle could make it but they made sure their own candidates passed and everybody else failed.

It turns out there is a reason why pilots and indeed navigators are chosen for their quick reaction times rather than their knowledge of Information Technology arcana and High Elvish folklore.

The Midgard, as far as we could tell, breached the gap between the parallel universes and brought us to this God-forsaken place. This was due to the brilliance of the mathematical model worked out by Grant and Owen. It would have won them a Nobel Prize had they been in the same universe as the Nobel Committee.

Then the ship went into an uncontrollable spin and spun into the ground. We had been wearing emergency suits in case of a loss of oxygen during the transition. These suits were uncomfortable so many of us hastened to take them off at the earliest opportunity. When the ship crashed, it was only those with emergency suits who survived with only superficial cuts and bruises. The others died. I have mixed feelings about Grant and Owen. Owen survived and Grant was one of the unfortunate ones. Grant had been the one who had produced the luger in my bedsit all those years ago.

The crew included a handful of engineers. The Inner Circle had regarded engineers as a very low form of life, just above politicians I imagine. However the engineers then had to teach the survivors their skills if we were to repair the Midgard or turn it into a habitable living space.

It was soon clear that we had nowhere near the number of skilled engineers or tools to get the Midgard up and running again. We had a plentiful supplies of copies of The Lord of the Rings and Silmarillion as well as DVD boxed sets of a passable film made by Peter Jackson. Spanners, screwdrivers and oscillators were as rare as hens' teeth unfortunately so the building of the town proceeded at a snail's pace. The core of the Inner Circle still hold meetings which are conducted entirely in Elvish but as far as I know nothing useful has so far come out of them.

What we have developed is a facility with languages. We have a positively Pentecostal ability to speak in tongues

24

and make ourselves understood by the local peasantry. We soon found out that they are just common or garden peasants. Here are no Rohirrim and there is nothing akin to the structure of Minas Tirith within striking distance of us. It is perhaps a disappointment with our own miscalculation which makes me so dismissive of the locals.

This is, after all, the first alien planet which human beings have made contact with. We soon found out that there is no practical way of communicating with Earth so the arrival of three travellers from Earth, albeit astral projections, is an important event. Wolf-Dietrich, Sister Lam and Xavier are too valuable to kill but then again Wolf-Dietrich was quick to prove that I had no way of doing so anyway.

Wolf-Dietrich is the most ghost-like of the three with his uncanny ability to disappear and walk through walls. Even the One Ring did not bestow that power. I have to constantly remind myself that this is RL *(Real Life – Narrator)* and not a work of fiction. It is ridiculous for a 17th Century Prince-Archbishop to be here but as Sister Lam insists, 'In your dreams you can go to any time or place.' I have not yet got to the bottom of the powers of Sister Lam and Xavier. Their mind-reading powers defy everything science knows about the mind and their strength seems to be equal to any task. They also seem to have some 'conjuring tricks' which they have learnt from Wolf-Dietrich and I will need to look out for them.

Xavier enlightens Elliott

Xavier stayed with Elliott while his companions went off to explore The Ship. Wolf-Dietrich and Sister Lam felt quite safe to explore. They reasoned that if the person who was in charge of prisoners could not kill them then neither could anyone else in The Ship. This proved to be the case.

They sat down for a chat.

""Do you remember your dreams?" Xavier asked.

"Fragments," Elliott said hesitantly, "Usually when I have been awakened by something or someone I will have a memory of being eaten by a giant spider or I might remember something scary from Eastenders."

"Remembering your dreams will be the first step to controlling them. For a start you will have to kill that giant spider by any means necessary."

"I can't do that." Elliott seemed shocked by the very idea.

"There is no such word as 'can't'," said Xavier, echoing the strictures of his mother, Geert. "You have to believe, Elliott,

26

that you can do anything in the dreamscape. In real life there are all kinds of restrictions on what you can do. In a short period of time you will find that in the dreamscape you can go anywhere and do anything. You cannot be killed.

"To be precise, your body here can be killed but your astral projection cannot be killed. Your astral projection will be more akin to Wolf-Dietrich's than to mine but I will pass on the 'conjuring tricks' which he has taught me."

"Why are you different?" Elliott wanted to know.

"I discovered, or Sister Lam would say that I 'stumbled upon', a means of making a hard astral projection. It involves some rather arcane practices which my father had been researching and it required The Mirror of Eternity."

"What is the Mirror of Eternity when it's at home?"

"I am surprised that the Inner Circle knew nothing of it. The Mirror of Eternity overcomes the paradoxes of time travel. It involves the use of some banned substances but it enables me to look into the past without interfering in the past. In fact I am unseen and unheard. Attempts by the security forces to replicate the action of the Mirror of Eternity have failed because their subjects, who were usually prisoners, were not receptive to the experience. They would not risk

27

any of their own people in this activity so they never found out if they were receptive or not.

"In addition the hard astral projection makes use of Terrence Hollands' research. My father searched out Black Magic folklore and picked through the stories. Satanists would usually use astral projection to interfere with their neighbour's ass in one way or another. Some of the folklore was just malicious so my father tried to sort the wheat from the chaff."

"Or the sheep from the goats." put in Elliott, "you know, the Goat of Mendes."

Xavier essayed a smile and continued, "Again the advantage of it is that it works. To be honest I have never experimented to find out which of the various rituals are necessary and which are not. I think there would be a certain risk with that."

"Risk?" Elliott asked.

"Well if I don't know which rituals are necessary, I do not know what the effect of cancelling one of them would be. I have had some bad trips with astral projections."

Seeing how crestfallen Elliott was, he quickly continued. "The thing to remember is that there is nothing to fear but fear itself. I must warn you that the fear is of a magnitude you have never encountered before. My spiritual mentor, Wolf-Dietrich, taught me how to master that fear and in time you could learn it too. And although you cannot report to the Science Minister, there must be a receptive member of the Inner Circle remaining in the UK that you could report to."

"To whom I could report." Elliott corrected smugly.

And from that day Elliott's adventures in the dreamscape began.

From the Diary of Elliott

There is a website which of course I cannot access called dreamcommand.blogspot.co.uk/ but Xavier has shared its secrets with me. The first part of the experiment was rocky. I remembered my dreams and noted them down but they were just an extension of my everyday life. Then one night I deliberately read about Samwise and his encounter with Shelob in *The Lord of the Rings* and ate a cheese sandwich. This last came from a bit of folklore than cheese would make you dream. Whatever the wrongs and rights of it, it worked.

The spider in my dreams was, if anything, worse than

anything I had seen before. It was huge and it had clustered eyes with a venomous glow to them. And in addition to the giant spider there were little blighters crawling all over me and biting my sword arm.

However I did have the sword and I was able to advance towards the lady of the darkness and put out one of her eyes with a well-aimed thrust. I felt that I did not have the strength for this fight but Xavier's advice sustained me. I had all the strength I needed. I cut off a number of legs. On reflection it was probably more than eight but the giant spider was disarmed by the time I had finished. I just wished the little biters away and away they went.

As a killer of a monster I felt ready for anything. I remembered that there was a girl I had been rather too wrapped up in myself to woo at Cambridge. Somehow, I found myself outside her door. I had gone back to my college days. I was not a boring old civil servant (I was a boring young student).

I will, as they say, draw a veil over what happened that afternoon. I did have a serious purpose here after all and she was not a member of the Inner Circle. The Inner Circle was exclusively male, as you might have guessed. There was also no point in haunting the dreams of Inner Circle

30

members before the launch of the Midgard.

Going forward to the present day, I went to the rooms of one Inner Circle member. He had been reluctantly excluded from the Midgard Project. I had to observe his dreams before I could make any attempt to talk to him. He was distracted.

Firstly he was engaged in imaginative and horrific ways of taking revenge on those who had been involved in the Midgard project. Naturally this included myself. In his dreams I had my eyes eaten out by worms I recall. That was unpleasant but it was as nothing to some of the punishments he wrought on Grant and Owen. Neither of them had much left in the genital area when he had finished with them.

Eventually he tired of this and I had to witness his sexual fantasies. He was certainly broad in his tastes and when I say I "had to" witness his sexual fantasies they were as good as a really sleazy DVD and I must admit that they momentarily distracted me from my task. In the dreamscape he was inexhaustible and he had no need of Viagra apparently.

There was a brief hiatus in which I was able to report my

findings to him. His response was a predictable incredulity. The Midgard had failed? Many of those he had been torturing in his imagination were in fact dead? It was too good to be true. And who would believe a bloody politician anyway?

He went off for more sexual romps and I had to possess my soul with patience for the rest of the night. As luck would have it, he had an afternoon nap the following day and I was able to catch him before he went off into the realms of fantasy torture and sex. I repeated my report.

"And I am expected to tell people you came to me in a dream with this?"

"Well I have thought about that. I think you should just produce a report and be cagey about the source. Members of the Inner Circle will have the report and initially they will be sceptical. Then I will reinforce my message with them."

He named the most important four members of the Inner Circle and that night I visited the first of them. It was a long job to get around all of them but it was quite interesting to see what kind of dreams they had and to take an appropriate opportunity to tell them about the alien world we had landed on. For example, one of them dreamed about

32

academic meetings. In his dreams he dominated these meetings. I suspect he did not do so in real life. I just turned up at one of these academic meetings and presented my report. He duly thanked me and went on to next business.

For good measure I did haunt the dreams of the Minister of Science but as Owen and Grant predicted he knew nothing about Midgard so the information was wasted. The Assistant Secretary to the Minister was a member of the Inner Circle. His dreams were entirely in the land of Tolkien's Middle Earth so my bulletin from the world of reality fell on deaf ears. I also tried a few astronomers but my facts did not fit their theories so it seemed as if only the Inner Circle would be receptive to the news of the greatest breakthrough in human exploration ever.

Whilst playing "The Lord of the Rings" board game with Xavier that night, I got to thinking about Gandalf. It seemed some of his exploits like escaping from Orthanc or rescuing the halflings in Mordor were accomplished with the aid of giant eagles.

"In your dreams, can you fly?" I asked.

Xavier, who was losing heavily, took a moment to reply.

"Some people can."

"Meaning?"

"Sister Lam. I don't know if Wolf-Dietrich has tried."

It came out that Sister Lam had been taught by a Doctor Katherine how to fly but she had adapted to Xavier's more pedestrian lifestyle.

"It would be an ideal way to spy out the land." I suggested.

"So it would. So it would." said Xavier absent-mindedly as he made another foolish move.

My first attempts at flying came after another visit to the student in Cambridge. I had better mention her name which was Clare. I do not intend to give any other details. I am not scripting a porn film after all.

I tried various methods but strangely enough it was when I was not thinking about flying but about how the ground would look from the sky that I had my breakthrough. Suddenly I was up above the clouds looking down through the gaps to see the landscape rolling away beneath me.

Initially I wondered how the peasants would take to the idea of a man flying. I certainly didn't want them to think I was a god or some kind of witch. And then it struck me. They could no more see me than they could see Wolf-Dietrich when he didn't want to be seen. At worst they might see a small cloud passing overhead.

I visited the nearest village. I confirmed that they use horses for ploughing and transport but they have nothing like the cavalry of the Rohirrim.

I went further afield and my journey was rewarded. There was a valley of wild horses. I circled the valley. The horses seemed vaguely aware of my presence and they were a little skittish as a result. As my circles became wider I saw a village which I thought might be promising so I landed to explore.

It is fair to say that this village had a cavalry of sorts and they had tamed some of the wild horses. Rohirrim? Well they might be in a century or so perhaps. However I overheard a scrap of conversation about "the little people" who lived far to the west of the village.

That was the point at which I realised two things. One was that I didn't know what "west" was and the second was that I had no way of getting back to The Ship. Further earwigging got me the answer to one of these. The sun was in every respect the same as our own sun as far as I could tell (I am not an astronomer). According to the local dialect it rose in the North.

I worked out where west was. I was rather proud of myself. And were there really 'little people' living there? Not a bit of it. Any difference in height between these people and the average peasant was slight. It was true that they were engaged in minor mining operations in the mountains but their lives were mainly agricultural. Their language was different but it was not harsher than the tongue of the local peasantry. It was if anything more musical to my untutored ear.

I went further west over the mountains and a large proportion of the land was unoccupied. The inhabitants were all men, I should say humans. Nothing resembling elves or dwarves let alone hobbits. The differences in size were largely exaggerations caused by distance. It was only when I settled down in gatherings of the people in market places, bars (I had to be careful not to spook the customers in bars) and around camp-fires that the real Midgard came to life for me.

The stories! The lives of these peasants seemed dull to me but their stories were peopled with elves, dwarves, gods and wizards. I sat and listened to many a story from the

36

village storytellers as well as itinerant storytellers who roamed from village to village and would exchange a tale for a night's bed and breakfast and the inevitable horn of ale of course.

I retraced my route and I found the village I had visited first. They were unusual in having a female storyteller. In their tales, their tiny cavalry could send hundreds of riders across the plain to vanquish their foes in bloody battle, In reality they got on quite well with their neighbours and had no foes to talk of.

She then began a story about Win. Win was obviously a popular character and I will set down here all I can remember of the tale.

Win's Tale

A girl called Win had forged a sword in secret in the woods. At this time there were rumours of a big cat which was driving the shepherds from the hills. The size of the cat grew in the telling but soon it was devouring sheep so it must have been fairly large. The warriors of the village would go out to fight the cat alone. This hunt for glory on their part prevented them from killing it. If they had gone out mob-handed they would have stood a chance. Singly they either came back badly mauled or they did not come back at all.

So one fine day, Win begged the task of vanquishing the cat.

"No maid may attempt this deed." was the decision of the elders.

Win just leant on her sword and looked at them. One by one their faces dropped and they mumbled their agreement.

Win set off the same day. She watched the cat from a safe distance. It was as black as midnight but its eyes and whiskers identified it as a cat. She watched and watched as the cat hunted down and killed a sheep. It grabbed the throat of the sheep and held on with its teeth until the sheep dropped to the ground. Then it wasted no time in devouring the sheep.

Win watched as the cat settled down to sleep. She approached it. She was very careful not to make a noise. It twitched in its sleep and Win stood stock still for a whole minute until she was sure it was asleep.

The cat opened its eyes but once but it was too late. Win's sword sliced through its neck with ease. She returned to the village with her sword still smoking with the blood of the cat.

"How do we know that she has slain the cat and not just wounded it?" one of the defeated warriors demanded to know.

Win just turned on her heel and set off back to the cat. Two hours later she arrived and threw the head of the cat at the feet of the warrior.

"And how come a mere girl could kill the cat when our greatest warriors (he clearly included himself in this category) have failed?"

"Well I waited until it was asleep and severed its head from its body."

"Well that is not how a warrior would behave. You cannot take unfair advantage of an opponent even if it is a cat."

"Well there is no problem," said Win, "the cat had a sister and I have left her to the brave warrior."

She handed her sword to the man. The whole village laughed when he refused it.

Later one of the women asked, "Aren't you going off to kill

the sister of the cat?"

"What sister?" said Win. "That was just a trick to show our mighty warrior up for a buffoon."

Elliott's return

In the end it was not necessary to find my way back to The Ship. I woke up there and immediately transcribed Win's story.

I submitted a report to the Inner inner circle committee. It was in perfect Elvish of course and I understand that they will consider it 'when time allows'.

I was in time for the return of Sister Lam and Wolf-Dietrich.

An extract from the Diary of Sister Lam

Well last things first. Elliott has found out that the people of this planet – as far as he has gone – are creating their own mythology. The attempt to find Middle Earth has succeeded from a certain point of view but the answer may not please the questioners.

And Wolf-Dietrich and I have found enough of the questioners to last us a lifetime. Elvish is an incomplete and artificial language and they had to substitute English words for many of the things they named. They did not see that this was ridiculous. Fortunately their thoughts were in English which simplified things for me if not for Wolf-Dietrich who regards English as a vulgar tongue.

We have explored the ship to the best of our ability and each time we had to explain our peaceful intentions to the inhabitants. Apparently Elliott had told them all about us but they distrusted him because he was a politician and they wanted to verify things for themselves.

At the centre of the innermost inner circle was an individual I like to think of as the Lord High Panjandrum . I found him tedious in the extreme but Wolf-Dietrich endured many hours of discourse with him. At the end of which he said,

"We will have some visitors who will please you today."

"And who might that be? I despise guessing games!"

"Mr and Mrs John Smith. They will be brought here in one of the few motor vehicles The Ship possesses. They are to start an adult school if they are willing. The school will teach the local peasants all the secrets of The Ship. It will advance their technology by several centuries."

"Is that a good thing?" I wondered.

"It is better than The Ship hogging its knowledge. I may

41

remind you that the peasants have a life-expectancy of fifty and the Ship men a life-expectancy of a hundred so there must be some value in their knowledge."

"How did you convince the Lord High Panjandrum to go along with this?"

"I flattered him mercilessly of course, Sister Lam. His sort can take any amount of flattery you know. As for you, you are honour-bound to love him and I hope you don't mind me reminding you."

If it is possible for Wolf-Dietrich to have a twinkle in his eye then take my word that he had one that day.

We roped Elliott and Xavier in to teach a few classes until that is it was time for us to depart. There were tears when I parted company with the Smiths and I think Xavier and Elliott will meet again in the dreamscape.

Wolf-Dietrich was keen to get back to his beloved Salzburg (and to his beloved Salome's bed) but Xavier and I had an appointment with a waterfall.

The second path

Relaxing by the waterfall, they took their time choosing between the second and third pathways. Eventually old-fashioned numerical order drove them to the second because using the third would seem like jumping the gun.

They walked hand-in-hand along the path through the forest. Acorns crunched underfoot. Xavier thought that it would be a hostage to fortune to wonder why it was never pouring with rain on these trips to the dreamscape. He was not wrong. The first heavy drop of rain fell on his nose. They trudged on through the forest and came quite soon to a cottage. They agreed to try to talk to the inhabitants and beg a bed for the night against the storm which had now developed.

The door was opened by a beaming woman in a plain dress with a couple of pegs attached to the front pocket as if she had expected to be putting out washing but had thought better of it.

"Ah Xavier and Tilly, or should I say Sister Lam?" was her surprising greeting.

"Sister Lam." came a male voice from within which seemed to ooze surliness.

"Well would you be wanting a bed for the night in this

43

horrible weather?" she asked as if reading their minds.

The surly voice had a face to match, Grim was the other half of the affable Gwen.

"I expect you're wondering how Gwen knew your names like. Well I better tell you Mr Smarty-Pants Xavier Hollands. Folks in this land can read minds as well as thee. I am Grim by the way."

Grim by name was Grim by nature. He must have realised that he was broadcasting far and wide his desire to murder and rob his guests but it did not seem to bother him one jot.

"Now what will it be. Leek and onion soup. Oh I am sorry. I see on the surface of your mind you have taken a vow to St Katherine to abstain from food but deep down I can see that you both fear that eating in what you call the Dreamscape will tie you to this reality for ever. Well this is not too bad a reality, young Xavier and Sister Lam as you will find when you venture onwards but I will respect your vow to St Katherine for now."

Grim and Gwen tucked in to the leek and onion soup. Grim ate with his mouth open and then picked his teeth with gusto.

Xavier and Sister Lam did not need to sleep in the double

44

bed Gwen provided them so that they were able to sense Grim's plots to kill and rob them as they seethed in his brain. In the end it got too much for him and a sudden knife came within inches of Xavier's chest. He grasped the wrist in a grip of iron and Grim cried aloud.

The cry awakened Gwen and she took the knife from his hand.

"How many times have I told you not to murder the guests," she admonished gently. "I really can't be doing with your doings. Now you apologise to Xavier."

Grim mumbled something which might have been an apology.

Xavier and Sister Lam were pleased to see the pale light of dawn.

As they set off on their journey, Gwen apologised again for Grim's 'wilfulness' adding 'There's no harm in him really."

She warned them that it was "a tidy step" from the cottage to the town and that proved to be true. They wondered how they would cope with a town of mind-readers.

"It might be fun." Sister Lam concluded.

"It might not." Xavier thought but he did not say it out loud.

45

The sun was shining when they arrived at the town. People in the street greeted them by name and appeared to be friendly. Underneath the friendliness however, there were rather more echoes of Grim's desire to kill and rob them than they had expected to see. There was no police force and it seemed that citizens were expected to anticipate trouble and avoid it.

As far as Xavier and Sister Lam could see the system seemed to work. The aggressive individuals realised they had no opportunity to unleash their aggression so had to restrain themselves.

Although they were not drinking they found inns congenial so they made for the Traveller's Rest. It was a quite civilised inn and there was a role for storytellers. Xavier told a tale from the Arabian Nights which went down well.

Next up was an old man who told a rambling tale and seemed to be unfocussed. Then there came a change, like a commercial break in the story, and there was nothing vague about the look he gave to Sister Lam and Xavier.

"Our new guests, Sister Lam and Xavier, have been invited to a meeting of the Elders." And two of the larger muscular townsmen rose from their seats to make sure the invitation was accepted. As they left, the old man was continuing with his tale.

Elders was a courtesy title. The council was roughly half male and half female and included young and old. They did not exactly question Sister Lam and Xavier. They were invited to sit in chairs and the Elders just waited.

They could feel their minds being probed by experts. They were pleased to see that the Council of Elders did not contain any of the Grim population. Their thoughts seemed benevolent for the most part. Some were taking notes.

Eventually one of the Elders, a woman in her thirties who was named Selena, stood and addressed Xavier out loud. "We can see that you are, in your terms, an astral projection, a hard astral projection. You have obtained this state by the use of the Mirror of Eternity. The Mirror of Eternity requires the use of drugs which we do not have and technological devices which we do not possess. We have computers but they are human beings not machines. We think you have trusted too much to machines which may not have your best interests at heart."

Another Elder continued, "In this reality, which you call the dreamscape, you are devotees of St Katherine. You have

47

both met St Katherine and Sister Lam was even trained by her. Your thoughts are also filled with Wolf-Dietrich von Raitenau. Is it possible to call him to this council?

"Better than that. I have taught one person how to navigate the dreamscape. If you are willing, Selena, then I could train you or another member of the Elders and then you can meet Wolf-Dietrich in person." Xavier offered.

"You refer to Elliott. I agree that if you can train him you can train anybody and I take the challenge."

Selena was a fast learner and it was within three days that she was ready for her voyage into the dreamscape.

Extract from Selena's Diary

The Prince-Archbishop Wolf-Dietrich von Raitenau lived in a male-dominated world and he was, on the face of it, an unpromising character to make contact with. For example he issued an edict banning the Jews (a religious and racial minority) from the state of Salzburg and he seemed obsessed with stopping the Bavarians and Austrians from dominating his domain.

I took Xavier's advice and followed Wolf-Dietrich into the dreamscape itself. I saw him visiting an obscure town to tell

48

stories to the children. I did notice that he used his stories to promote "X" as a saviour to these people. A fairly obvious reference to Xavier.

Then he visited the town many years later and I witnessed a big change of heart as he used his considerable political skills to help Krystyna to power as leader of the town. And I saw him help the Miranda revolution to victory.

Then it became time for us to meet properly. From Xavier's description I realised that it was the graveyard of St Sebastian and I could only imagine that the monument to bad taste at the centre was the mausoleum of Wolf-Dietrich. There was no sign of the man himself. As Xavier had said, I could feel no cold but there was a light mist obscuring my vision. I had the strange experience of putting my foot directly through a gravestone which I cannot recommend. As I was retrieving my foot, Wolf-Dietrich appeared.

"Are you an adept of the left-hand path?" he asked out loud.

"No I am not, as well you know."

"Do you fear the spirits of the dead might impede your progress?"

"Wolf-Dietrich, you can read my mind as easily as I can read yours so these questions are in vain."

49

"You have mind-reading skills but you are not an adept..."

"of the left-hand path, whatever that is. I was born telepathic. Everyone I know was born telepathic. It's the reason we never play card games or dominoes."

"Very well, Selena, you will have your wish.

"You mean."

"I will come to meet your council of Elders."

From the Diary of Wolf-Dietrich

The meeting with the council of Elders was more like a trial to start with. They brought up a number of things from my past and indeed present role as Prince-Archbishop of Salzburg which were, as I said, nobody's business but my own.

After consulting with Xavier and Sister Lam I was able to draw their attention to a clear and present danger which they were failing to deal with.

"There are people in this town, Xavier has called them 'The Grims' who harbour the most violent thoughts."

"We know," said Selena who seemed to be the nearest thing the elders had to a leader, "and the citizens control their violent urges. We have a democratic system here. The elders are elected by all of the people, including those you label as 'Grim', and they have very sensibly not elected any violent people to this body."

"Very sensibly, you say. I wonder if we mean the same thing by that. How long do you think it will take the Grims to organise themselves into a body to wage war on the elders? Given your telepathic abilities they would very sensibly not have any representatives on the Elders who might give away their plans.

"I can see that you wonder that people as enlightened as you can learn anything from an old autocrat like me. I can only say with all modesty that I only state the obvious. I could almost say that you are too nice for your own good."

This put the Elders onto a new track and they entered into a discussion about how to deal with the Grims. In the first place they had no weapons. In the second place they could not forge weapons in secret because the Grims could read their minds.

It is a simple trick to fill the surface of your mind with a well-remembered form of words. Your enemy will know you are concealing something but they will not know what that

51

something is. I taught the Elders how to do this and in the process I taught them the Lord's Prayer which cannot have done them any harm.

Afterwards some of them stayed behind to learn what the Lord's Prayer meant and Xavier and Sister Lam were eager to help me explain. They have lost none of their enthusiasm those two.

Sister Lam, Xavier and I then held a meeting of minds to co-ordinate the battle against the Grims. Much time was expended on the making of weapons. We rejected the idea of a sweep of the town to capture the weapons of the Grims because that would only alert them to our preparations and that would be fatal.

"Are we assuming that the Grims will make a frontal assault on the Elders? Will they not seek to take the centres of communication, the TV station for example?" asked Xavier.

"Well the locals don't watch TV, they make their own fun." said Sister Lam.

"What do they use as their source of news?" Xavier asked.

"Like us, they use radio. And the Elders aren't daft. The only radio station is right here in the Elders' meeting house. They don't control..."

"They claim they don't control," Wolf-Dietrich added.

"They claim they don't control the editorial content." Sister Lam emended, "but the practical upshot of this is that the most likely assault from the Grims will be on this building. They may have been able to improvise an explosive device or they may use the conventional weapons of this era – knives and swords."

"Defending against a bomb is more difficult but it is more likely that the bomb will destroy the bombers. This is inevitable because the Grims have, as far as we know, no experience of making bombs. You must remember that the Grims are not terrorists. They are criminals. They will not engage in suicide attacks. Still the Elders should organise a rota to keep eyes on the streets around this building in case my guess about a bomb is wrong." Xavier's thought got the agreement of the others and I took the first opportunity to tell Selena about it. Her decisive response impressed me. She definitely has the leadership qualities I have always suspected she possessed.

Within 24 hours Selena's guards were discretely positioned around the building. I was pleased to hear their minds dutifully repeating the Lord's Prayer. Using the words would make them think about the meaning of the words. I was confident that would draw them towards Jesus Christ. The Lord's Prayer can never be treated as empty words. It is too powerful for that.

A Grim battle

The Lord's prayer certainly caused a lot of conversation among the elders. Should they defeat the Grims by loving them or defeat them first and love them afterwards? In the event the attack of the Grims caught them by surprise although thanks to Wolf-Dietrich they were expecting it.

The radio station for the town was located on the top floor of the building and unsurprisingly they had all (including Xavier) been expecting an attack at ground level. They had reckoned without the ingenuity of the Grims. Although the adjacent buildings were not very close to the Elders' Meeting House, the Grims had secretly brought ladders which they used to make a daring raid on the radio station.

"They have taken the top floor." Xavier said.

"Who?" "What?" "When?" The Elders were in a pickle of confusion. Only Selena had a level head and immediately took steps to secure the lower floors and sent people to the basement where spare radio equipment was stored. There they were able to rout a small group of Grims who had attacked simultaneously using the sewers as an entrance.

They were also able to rig up a radio station of sorts. It had to broadcast on a different frequency and the town radios were not always equipped for more then one frequency. Still it was better than nothing.

Xavier was in charge of monitoring the Grim radio broadcasts. They were proclaiming a change of government in between the music programmes which, to Xavier's ear, sounded quite good. Reports reaching the Elders' Meeting Hall by messengers spoke of a wholesale slaughter being carried out systematically by the Grims. These reports hardened the resolve of the Elders. They would try their hardest to love the Grims but they would defeat them first. By any means necessary.

An assault on the Radio Station seemed to be ruled out. It could only be reached by two staircases and the Grims had an inbuilt advantage against any opponent who was trying to climb them.

The solution to this problem came from an unexpected source.

"Gas and gas masks." was all Sister Lam said but Selena caught on immediately. The gas need not be fatal. It merely needed to incapacitate the Grims for long enough for an attack up one staircase and a feint up the other to succeed. The gas masks need not be complicated, just smog masks would do. The reports of mass killing in the town were enough to sing the consciences of the Elders to sleep.

The elders had "alternates" - people who could stand in for Elders who were unfit for duty – and these were called into play now. Without explanation they were sent into the town to obtain the chemicals needed to create the tear gas and the material to make smog masks. Smog was unknown in the town. Their qualifications as "alternates" clearly included an ability to obey without question. Not knowing the facts they could not pass on the information to the Grims though they might trigger speculation.

The Elders had an assortment of knives but few swords. Xavier bagged one ceremonial sword which was engraved with the names of illustrious male Elders and Sister Lam, rather unusually for a nun, bagged the one with the few names of illustrious female Elders. Clearly the Elders had been an equal opportunity body for a brief time.

They practised in the basement where they hoped the

56

sound would not carry to the upper floors. Sister Lam matched Xavier stroke for stroke and eventually disarmed him. As his sword clanged on the stone floor, he tried to feel good about this.

"I was going to suggest you lead the feint up the north staircase. I now think I might take that job if you will lead the main assault up the south staircase.

"As usual your ideas of north and south are completely out to lunch but I am pleased to accept the position. I will lead the charge of the monstrous regiment of women – Selena will be at my right hand – and we will put the Grims to the sword or knife or hammer as the case might be.

"You know the hammer is a damned fine weapon, especially the no-nonsense clump hammer which can bring down walls if need be and the Grims ought to fear it. I will hold on to the sword of honour as I have it in my hand."

"Do you think a sister of the order of St Katherine ought to carry a sword?"

"Under normal circumstances no. These are not normal circumstances. The Elders are resolved to fight the Grims and it would be the part of a craven to desert them." Sister Lam grinned.

"I am resolved to love the Grims when they have been defeated and to keep the killing to a minimum. Is that good enough for you?"

Xavier spread his hands in a gesture which could have meant anything. Then he embraced and kissed Sister Lam in a gesture which was unequivocal.

The Elders looked sinister in their smog masks which were made of various materials in various colours but predominantly black. The tear gas was fed into the air-conditioning system and Sister Lam and Xavier blew whistles to signal the assault up the staircases. It was not an easy fight but the Grims were incapacitated as Sister Lam had anticipated and easy prey to the sword or the knife or, as Sister Lam noted, the hammer.

The hammer blows broke limbs rather than killing outright and although the Grims thus afflicted made a terrible fuss they were much better off then the ones who were silent because of a knife or sword thrust which had taken their lives.

Sister Lam noted but did not comment on the fact that the Grims who had stormed the radio station were all male.

She concentrated on nursing the injured and in salving their wounds she liked to think that she salved her conscience a little. She had taken no lives in the conflict but dealt out some vicious injuries. She treated them first.

Taking control of the radio station, Selena made a broadcast.

"We have for many years had people in our midst who harbour violent thoughts. We have restrained them with love and understanding. If you are still able to do so then by all means do so.

"There has been a change in the situation. The violent ones have formed an army and launched an attack on the elected Council of Elders. We have beaten off their first attack and to do so we have had to use violence. This is contrary to our nature as it is contrary to yours.

"However, the Elders are now calling for the formation of street committees for self-defence. The street committees will defend the citizens from any attack. They are only to act in self-defence. In your cupboards or sheds you will have hammers. In your kitchens you will have knives, sharp knives. These will do for defence for starters.

"Xavier, a traveller, will be giving you instruction in the use of the quarterstaff. If you want to know what a quarterstaff is, take the brush off the end of your ordinary house broom and you have a quarterstaff. Again, the methods which Xavier will talk to you about are only to be used for self-defence.

"Many citizens have been slaughtered by the devotees of violence and we will not permit this to continue. We will defend our citizens as we have defended the Elders' Meeting House to recapture the radio station. We give warning to any devotees of violence that the hammer of retribution is waiting for them if they continue these foolish attacks. That is not a metaphor. Many of the attackers are having their wounds from hammer blows dressed as I speak.

"This is Selena, speaking from the recaptured radio station in the Elders' meeting hall."

The next attack from the Grims was at ground level and the attackers could politely be described as a rabble. The confidence of the Elders grew as they beat this wave into submission.

"The Grims have made an elementary error," said Wolf-Dietrich. "They sent their leadership group into the first assault and there is only the riff-raff to continue the fight.

60

Leading from in front is all very heroic but it does have that unfortunate effect."

When the battle was won, the trio were keen to leave Selena in charge of the war. They thought that this would build her self-confidence.

Wolf-Dietrich was also keen to get back to his beloved Salzburg. Nevertheless he spent many hours discussing with Selena. At the end of the discussion, he baptised her. She had thought a small ceremony with just Xavier and Sister Lam present would be appropriate. Wolf-Dietrich persuaded her that the whole Council of Elders should witness her baptism and she agreed.

The ceremony knit the council of Elders together as never before. The transformation was a sight to see. They were decisive. They were of one mind (and to be honest It was usually Selena's mind) and they were a fighting force ready to face the remnants of the Grims.

Sister Lam embraced Selena on their parting, as did Xavier. Wolf-Dietrich was more restrained but his farewell was no less heart-felt.

The Third Path

Xavier and Sister Lam returned to the waterfall. They were reluctant to take the third path and they spent longer than usual chatting and exchanging thoughts about their experiences.

In the end they took the third path.

The woods began to fade away on either hand and gave way to tilled land. There were fields of barley and rye and rapeseed. Their only concern was to avoid trampling the crops as city-dwellers tend to do.

They kept to the hedge sides and made good progress. When they came to a farmhouse they did not debate long over whether to beg a bed for the night. Their experience of Gwen and Grim had taught them to be wary of cottages.

They carried on to the nearest village. To their surprise there was a church dedicated to St Katherine. They went into the cool darkness to pay their respects to the Saint and to pray to God.

On leaving they saw a beggar hiding in the portico. Xavier went off to find himself an afternoon's work with a carter and earn two pennies. He came back and gave it to the beggar and Sister Lam was able to match it. Answering Xavier's look she said, "I begged alms."

It was time for the evening service but the sermon rather surprised them.

The priest was a Father Colm and his text was the story of the Good Samaritan.

"Now I spied two of our flock who probably thought they were acting like the Good Samaritan this evening. They were giving money to the beggar at our gates.

"Was this beggar a good man?"

The congregation answered as one voice, "No!"

"No indeed. On the contrary the man is a drunkard and a ne'er-do-well. Did the members of our flock inquire what this evil man would do with their hard-earned cash? No they did not. We have a poor box, it is a box for the deserving poor, and I can assure you that the board of charity takes great care to see that only the deserving poor get that money.

"I hope our newcomers will have the sense to pay into the poor box and not help these unworthy individuals."

Xavier muttered quietly, "whatsoever you do to even the

least of our brethren, you do it to me."

The congregation and priest were scandalised to find as they exited the church that Sister Lam was busy washing the feet of the beggar.

"Oh, St Katherine, the things that are being done in thy name." was all she would say to the passers-by.

To Xavier she said, "we cannot allow this to continue."

From Father Colm's Diary

Tonight I was vouchsafed a vision of St Katherine. She appeared to me in the form of a statue in the church but then she subtly changed into what I might describe as a more realistic woman. I was sure it was still St Katherine. I fell to my knees and I started to tell her of the good works I had been doing for the deserving poor but one look from her silenced me and a gesture of her hand told me to rise up and follow.

She took me to the portico of the church where that pesky drunk had deposited himself again. I was on the verge of telling her that this was not how I wanted visitors to her church to be greeted when she knelt down and started washing his feet. Where she got the water from I do not know. It just appeared as is the way of things in dreams.

"If you don't want to give him money because he might spend it on booze then at least fetch some food from the presbytery kitchen." was the Saint's instruction to me.

I went to the presbytery and made a sandwich. I noticed as if for the first time that there was plenty of food in this kitchen. There was rather more food than one man needs really. And I felt something. It must have been the influence of the Saint but I felt that somehow I was like the drunk in the portico, that we had a common humanity and I had been, well the best word would be obnoxious, towards this man.

I brought the food. St Katherine had vanished by now but I gave it to the beggar anyway.

Then everything changed. Somehow I changed places with the beggar. Suddenly I felt as if I had slept on stone for days on end, I had a terrible thirst for alcohol and I was hungry. I will not conceal the fact that I felt sorry for myself. I could scarcely stand and every part of my body was aching.

I knew, because all my companions had been drunks, that I was killing myself by degrees and I would be very lucky to reach the grand old age of sixty. My father had drunk himself into an early grave at 56 and my mother at 59. There was always drink in the house but at least we had a house. My dad managed to keep a job despite his drinking habit. His employers were tolerant and he always turned up, drunk or sober, on time for his work.

There was no hope in my life but the wine could ease the pain for a while. How I longed for that wine! It was as if alcohol was giving the orders and I was just obeying.

I heard a bell ringing and by degrees I realised that it was my alarm clock. I was very pleased to wake up in my own bed. I dressed in haste and went out to the portico to see if the beggar was still there. He was gone and for the first time in my life, I wondered where he went.

Extract from Sister Lam's Diary

Perhaps all saints are blessed with a sense of humour. I am glad that Saint Katherine is. Last night I invaded the dreams of Father Colm. He may see it as a vision from Saint Katherine and indirectly it is. I have planted in his mind the idea of searching out where the beggar in the portico goes. If he does not follow it up, I will repeat his vision for him until he does.

I have persuaded Xavier to trace the beggar with me. At first he did not believe that "we" had the power to influence someone's dreams. To be honest I am not sure that "we" do. This would be one of the "conjuring tricks" that Wolf-Dietrich did not teach him.

We started out from the portico of Saint Katherine's after morning mass. We kept a discreet distance as the beggar, whose name was Maur, made his slow unsteady way. He made straight for the Bluebell Inn, a rather down-at-heel tavern which served cheap wine. He couldn't afford a whole bottle but he bought a glass of red.

Xavier and I went in and bought a meal, a mushroom salad, we went to sit with Maur.

"Do you remember us?" I asked.

He was immediately defensive. He did not like being asked questions.

"We are sharing a meal. Would you like to share it with us?" Xavier asked.

Maur took a mushroom and eyed it suspiciously. Then he ate it and took another and another until he had cleared the plate. If he noticed we had not eaten anything he didn't mention it.

He was making his glass of wine last as long as possible but he knew it would not be able to satisfy him. There are advantages in reading the mind of someone who is not drunk. Drunks can scarcely read their own minds. Maur's thoughts, although muddled, were not incoherent.

"F*cking bastard!" he ventured at last. We didn't need to ask who the "F*cking bastard" was because the face of Father Colm was plain in Maur's mind, although Maur did not know his name.

"Why do you say that?" asked Xavier.

"Because he is a f*cking bastard!" Maur's voice was getting louder and people in the Inn were looking around to see what the fuss was about. The barman was making moves preparatory to throwing Maur out, as he had done many times before.

I tried my best to calm him down. At first he repeated the phrase louder, then quieter and eventually he said, "I know full well why nobody, well almost nobody, at that bloody Church will give me anything. It is because of that...man."

"Have you tried anywhere else?"

"Well I have tried the market place and I have tried here, though the landlord does not like it. I have scraped together a few pennies and sometimes someone will buy me a drink." At this point he looked hopefully at Xavier who slowly shook his head.

"Sometimes I collect glasses at the Rook Tavern for pennies from the barman. I haven't tried it here where the landlord has taken a dislike to me. I only drink here because it is the cheapest in town.

"The thing is, I was raised a good Catholic. Well perhaps you could make that a bad Catholic. My parents took me to mass and made sure that I went even when they didn't. The times I went on my own became more and more frequent. Dad was often too hung-over to go. I believed that Christians had to help the poor. Not the **deserving poor."** He spat the expression out like an obscenity.

"Where does the Bible talk about 'the deserving poor' I'd like to know. 'Pauperem dignum" I have heard the word of God many times but those two words didn't come up."

"They don't." I assured him "and if you can stop calling him a 'f*cking bastard' then Xavier and I are going to have a go at changing his mind. How about that?"

"I do remember you. You weren't like the others. You even came out and washed my feet. That is something I do remember from the bible. God bless you. And I wish you luck with that...man."

We accompanied Maur to the market place. People there knew him. Some scowled, some smiled but very few were giving him cash. ""Get a job!" was the refrain of the scowlers and I thought about what kind of job Maur could manage and if there was work available. It was easier for Xavier because he was young and (in the dreamscape at least) remarkably strong so I was not surprised the carter would give him an afternoon's work for a pittance.

In the end Maur made his way to the Rook Tavern and started collecting glasses. He was eventually repaid by the bartender with a glass of wine. From the expression on his face, it was not the best wine, although it might possibly be useful for removing varnish.

He then made his way back to St Katherine's in time for evensong. We invited him to come inside but he was not ready for that yet.

We went inside and when the time came for the Gospel reading it was the story of the prodigal son (If any readers do not know this one, Wolf-Dietrich would advise you to go to church more often but equally you can Google it). At the end of the reading, Father Colm got up to speak.

"The parable of the prodigal son can be viewed in many ways. The prodigal son's behaviour was disgraceful and the behaviour of his brother was exemplary. Yet the father's immediate response to the prodigal son was forgiveness.

"And don't we all need forgiveness? The church is like a hospital for sinners. When you confess your sins you receive absolution. God forgives you your sins through mother Church. I myself go to confession with a fellow priest. You will remember the woman who was taken in adultery and our Lord's instruction, 'Let he who is without sin cast the first stone.' Nobody cast the first stone because there was nobody without sin.

"Let me ask the same question to you. Will he or she who is without sin put their hand up?"

There was a nervous silence as every hand in the church completely failed to go up.

"And I do not put my hand up either. Let us say the Hail Mary together,

"Hail Mary full of Grace,

Blessed art thou among women,

71

And blessed is the fruit of thy womb, Jesus,

Holy Mary, mother of God,

Pray for us sinners,

Now and at the hour of our death."

I entered the father's dreams that night. It was one thing to confess he was a sinner. It was another to confess he was wrong.

From the diary of father Colm

I can be sure that this vision came from Saint Katherine because again she led me to the beggar, I learn his name is Maur, and again I was quite literally put into his situation. I felt I had to walk a mile in his shoes.

I went to the market place. There were people who would smile but give no money. They were poor enough themselves perhaps and couldn't afford to waste money on a drunk. There were people who would scowl and tell me to "get out of the way" or "get a job". That was hard because I had tried every trade in the village and they had all turned me down. Even the taverns had turned me down.

When I looked at it objectively of course I realised that if I had turned up sober and smartened myself up a little then I

72

would have stood a better chance. And at the same time I realised it could not be. I had an overwhelming thirst for wine (or beer or spirits if no wine were available) and I knew that I had descended to theft in the past to slake that thirst.

My life was heading on a downward spiral. There was no hope. I would end up in an early grave. And beyond the grave, what then? I would burn in a Hell of my own making.

But, by Saint Katherine this was ridiculous talk. "For the wretched of the earth there is a hope that never dies." I have heard that phrase often enough but it had a real meaning today. Nobody is beyond redemption. Kicking the alcohol habit would be tough. My raging thirst for the poison told me that. I could not hope to do it on my own. I needed the help of a power greater than myself. Let's cut the cackle and call it God.

And then of course it was borne in on me with a crushing force. How had mother church treated me? I was rejected, spurned and called 'undeserving' when all the time it was the guidance of Jesus that I needed. How could I seek it from a church which treated me so badly?

From the diary of Sister Lam

One thing Father Colm did have was authority. When he arrived at the Portico before Mass and told Maur to follow him, Maur followed. Maur told us later that he had been taken to the Presbytery and given soap and a towel. He was then dressed in borrowed clothes and given breakfast.

Father Colm accompanied him to the Church. He objected to sitting in the front row but was content to sit with Xavier and myself.

The homily was interesting.

"Mea culpa, mea culpa, mea maxima culpa. Through my fault, through my fault, through my most grievous fault. How many times do we say that and how many times must God wait in vain for us to realise what we are saying? I have blamed my neighbour when I should have forgiven him. I have said he is undeserving when that is not my decision to make. God says all the poor are deserving and I was wrong to say otherwise.

"I hope you will all welcome Maur into our community. There is more joy in heaven over one sinner who repenteth than over ninety nine righteous people who do not need to repent. And how much joy over a priest who admits he was

74

wrong? I don't know. Probably a lot."

At the end of mass Maur could not move for the well-wishers offering help and money and there was one offer of a job at a chandler's. Xavier and I quietly slipped away. We felt our work here was done. And Xavier was kind enough to say that as usual I had done most of the work and he had just been along for the ride.

We soon returned to the waterfall and tarried a while before taking the path back to real life. We enjoyed the field of wild flowers and picked up our problems light-heartedly when we rejoined the path. We had learned that although we thought we had problems, compared with Maur for example we did not have any.

Soon I was back in the pentacle and the reassuring warmth of Xavier's body was next to mine. Our adventure in the dreamscape was over. For now.

The death of Xavier's parents

Everything was grey. Although Xavier's eyes were open they might just as well have been closed. He could see a uniform grey without form or substance. He was lying on a very cold pavement. He was shivering. He was 7 years old and helpless.

He could hear the sound of traffic splashing through the slush. His 7-year-old self did not know that his parents had been killed, just that they were not there. His dreaming self did though and the sadness washed over him.

Of all the moments in time and space he could visit, this was the one he avoided. He had discussed it with Tilly. She supported Xavier's decision but she knew in her heart of hearts that one day he would be unable to resist the investigation.

She also knew that when that day came, she would be with him all the way. He did not have to face this alone. She started quietly doing her own research. She and Xavier loved each other so they could see what was going on in each other's minds. He knew what she was doing but he didn't inquire too closely.

The date, time and place were matters of public record. The involvement of the Satanist grand master known as Doctor Love was a matter only Xavier and Tilly knew about.

His parents were John Pollard and Mary Heath. They both came from Streatham and they had met at the Locarno ballroom.

John practised dancing during the week with the aim of impressing Mary on a Saturday night. Money was tight but he was prepared to do without in the week to splurge it all on a Saturday.

They were both inhibited individuals but John had a meeting with a man known only as Victor which might put an end to all that.

Victor looked a bit out of place in the cafe where they met. He wore an old-fashioned suit and tie and it was not a suit and tie venue, more of a lorry drivers' pull-up. It was called the Rumbling Tum and the tea came with globules of fat swimming in it. Victor just left his on the table and concentrated on John.

"You hinted at our last meeting that you might er..."

"...be able to help you seduce Mary?" Victor completed the thought.

"Well I wouldn't put it like that."

"Oh. Then I can't help you." Victor smiled. "Unless you want her to obey your every whim then I have no help to give you. You have to be strong and I have a tiny little pill which will help."

The Locarno was awash with "tiny little pills" but the rumour was that Victor's were the real deal and the rest were just trash.

John was a clerical assistant in the Social Security Office in Streatham. He handed over the best part of a month's salary for one of Victor's little pills.

"In a break in the music, you must put this in Mary's drink and make sure you have somewhere to take her right away. You have to seize the moment. Do not hesitate or allow your scruples to get in the way." There was a look on Victor's face which John did not like but he had just spent a lot of money on this and anyway he loved Mary, didn't he? He just wanted to break her inhibitions.

It was as though Victor saw through all this talk of love and could see John's basest instincts using love

78

as an alibi.

Saturday night came around and to John's surprise when he took Mary to the bar, Victor was just contriving to leave and patted him on the shoulder for luck. What he didn't notice was that the packet of three Durex had gone missing from his inner pocket and he would have to carry on regardless.

"What would you like?"

"Gin and It."

Palming the pill into the glass was child's play although to be fair John had been practising all week with an aspirin.

"Ooh I feel a bit funny."

"It's OK, Mary, come with me. I have a room just up the road where you can lie down for a bit. Would you like that?"

Mary was a virgin but the little pill had taken away all her inhibitions and she really loved John and was happy to open her legs for him.

They had sex (or made love) three times. He would have used up all his condoms if they had not unaccountably vanished.

They got dressed and John walked her to her home like a gent.

Victor caught up with John the next day.

"You must roger that filly again."

"I beg your pardon."

Victor repeated himself with relish. "She has given you her cherry now and it is up to you to keep her. You do love her, don't you?" and there was undisguised mockery in his question.

John nodded.

"Then from now on it is every night, whatever other things she has to do, however tired she is. And did you use a rubber johnny?"

"No."

"Good. Get her good and pregnant and she is yours for life, John. You ought to thank me."

It just so happened that Victor owned a property which he could see his way clear to renting to the happy couple. The rent was steep but Victor had a hold over John. Every time he looked at him or accidentally brushed his hand against John's groin it was as if he were saying 'I know things about you

John. I know your secrets."

The flat was built of cheap material but there were four expensive items. In the corners of the bedroom were concealed cameras. In Victor's flat in the next street, he brought together selected friends to watch TV. It was not Nationwide or Coronation Street. It was the John and Mary Show.

This was usually a curtain-raiser to a special kind of meeting for Victor's friends.

"I've invited old Vic round to tea on Friday." John announced.

"John! I wanted it to be just us. You know we need some time alone together. It's Friday night."

"Well, we owe him a lot. He found us this flat and he has been very helpful."

"I know, John, but," she lowered her voice, "I'm sorry. I know he is your friend but he gives me the heebie-jeebies. I don't like the way he looks at me."

"The way he looks at you?"

"Like he is undressing me and thinking of unspeakable things."

"Unspeakable things!" John was laughing.

81

Mary subsided. John tried to lighten the mood.

"Some of the paperwork came through today and you will never guess what old Victor's real name is."

"Sylvester?"

Mary was trying to match John's mood.

"Love!" said John, "Doctor Love."

"Doctor Lurve," Mary laughed.

"The Love Doctor!"

"I wonder if he is a real doctor."

"Hardly, "John contended, "If he wants to look at your appendix you should make an excuse and decline."

"And you don't mind him coming."

"Of course not. It is hard enough to get a doctor to make house calls these days."

"I bet they took the piss out of him at school. There was a boy at my school called Pretty and did he get fed up with it by the end."

So the good Doctor duly came for tea.

John could see nothing untoward about the way he looked at Mary.

That may have been because when John was watching he was propriety itself but Mary surprised some evil looks when John was out of the room for a moment.

Victor had brought a bottle and after the chicken and chips they settled down to some serious drinking.

Maybe there was something in the wine. Maybe there was some other reason but they conversation soon became strange.

Oddly Mary, who would have blushed and changed the subject, found she was quite passive.

Victor urged them to tell him all about their sex life and bit by bit they revealed more and more of themselves.

Victor looked at them with those hypnotic eyes and he talked about orgies. It seemed strange at first to have an old man relishing sex but after a while they were less inhibited and listened intently, getting sexually aroused.

"Of course getting an invitation to an orgy is the tough bit." He concluded.

"You mean..you mean you've been to one?" John

stammered.

An orgy was something which happened while normal people were reading the News of the World in those days.

"If you are interested, I will see what I can do. Save your pennies though."

When Victor left they both quite naturally embraced him. John was just suddenly fond of this old man. Mary likewise but she definitely felt something nasty and exciting in his embrace.

Tilly had to do a lot of to-ing and fro-ing and Xavier could not help but notice. The reason was that although Tilly knew Victor Love was an organiser of weekly orgies, the doctor wanted to impress on Mary and John just how difficult it was to get in. And of course this would help him to jack up the price he would charge them. As with the little pills, they were cheap to make but he sold them for a high price. This was partly greed and partly so that the punters would think they were getting "something special."

The men were of various ages but Victor made sure there were a good number of young girls. He picked them up off the streets with a bit of banter and an

84

apparently open palm. They were paid for their services in some cases but not a fraction of what he was making.

So Tilly visited Victor and the happy couple periodically but caught no hint of the time and place they would be invited to the orgy. She attended a lot of orgies as a vicarious observer and she knew that one day she would tell Xavier all about them, just not yet.

Other work on the Mirror of Eternity was building up but she coped.

The orgies, Victor was confident, Mary could cope with. He had been tutoring John in techniques for long enough to know what she could manage. He was not sure that the Satanism would exactly appeal.

It was a month after he first floated the idea that he was able to drop a hint to John who immediately invited him round for a meal.

Mary was quite acquiescent by this time. She would go along with whatever the men decided. She had other things on her mind.

Victor went out of his way to compliment her on how feminine and sexy she looked in her pregnant state. It would not be a problem at the orgy. It would just make her more attractive.

Tilly also saw him instructing his acolytes in how to treat the new members.

"This child is very important to us." was all he would say and he responded to any questions with a look which said "who is the Grand Master here?"

Tilly watched as Victor calibrated the cameras in his own home prior to the black mass and orgy. He intended to have a full record in case Mary or John should ever backslide. Blackmail is certainly one way to keep a Satanic order in check.

The mass was perfunctory and performed naked. Mary and John had never been to church and the ritual meant nothing to them. The orgy was beyond their expectations and Tilly reflected that it was just as well Victor used a powerful carpet shampoo.

John and Mary's regular attendance was cut short because of the birth of the child. He was called Xavier because Mary had heard the name somewhere and thought it was pronounced "Exavier"

They were able to go to one or two orgies after Xavier was safe to be left with babysitters. Jack was keen

86

and Mary was docile. Using the arts of Victor, John became the dominant partner for the time being.

You might wonder who would babysit a small child so the parents could go to a Satanic orgy.

Jenny, the charming woman who took on this role claimed she was getting too old for orgies. She was in her early forties. Her aversion to orgies was a complete fake , she relished them. Indeed, Tilly had seen her coaching young girls at Victor's orgies in how to perform. She also claimed that she had never been much of a Satanist. A bit of research told Tilly that Jenny had read more of the arcana than anyone with the possible exception of Victor. It was hard to say with Victor because he always asserted his male superiority. Women might read more but as a man he insisted he understood more. In fact Jenny had been hand-picked by Victor for this role.

Tilly gave the orgies a miss on three occasions over a period of four years. She focussed on Jenny and the young Xavier instead. In the Mirror of Eternity she achieved all of this in half an hour, completed her notes and still joined Xavier for a drink in Ye Olde Boar.

Initially, Jenny would bath and change Xavier and then she would sit in the nursery smoking cigarette after cigarette while he slept. She would watch his eyeball movements closely and recite arcane formulae to the dreaming Xavier to drill them into his unconscious mind and she would draw mystic signs on his skin with her fingernail, carefully leaving no marks.

By the second visit an older Xavier was learning portions of the black mass by heart and swearing to keep the whole thing "our secret". He said this as if Jenny were sexually abusing him. There was no evidence that she was. She was however grooming him for Victor.. The magic number of 7 was to be the age at which Victor Love planned to seduce Xavier. He planned to do so in order to bring Xavier over fully to the Satanic lifestyle. He was not to know that the adult Xavier spent much of his life as a floating voter sexually.

Geert, Xavier's adoptive mother, had found he periodically got portions of the mass perfectly back to front and she had to re-educate him. Xavier let out this piece of information to Tilly because it would never had occurred to Geert to tell Tilly. If she could avoid telling anything to her daughter-in-law at all she did so,

The final session saw Xavier playing with Jenny. It was not a nursery game but a nasty game of dominance and submission. Jenny accompanied it with laughter and songs to make it easier for Xavier but there was a hard look on her face as she forced him to submit over and over again.

There came a time when John and Mary could not afford their lifestyle. The rent was crippling and the orgies were setting them back more than they were earning. With a smile, Victor produced what he called a 'freeloader' contract which bound them to the "Streatham Esoteric Society" for life. The Streatham Esoteric Society was a limited company which was the public face of Satanism.

On a whim, Victor got them to sign in their own blood. The wording was quaint. "I commit my body and soul as far as it is in my power to do so to the Streatham Esoteric Society (hereafter SES), its heirs and successors. I undertake not to violate any instruction I may receive from the SES or to reveal such instructions to any tertium quid (an old legal term for

89

"third party". John and Mary did not know what it meant and didn't like to ask). I do solemnly swear this insofar as it concurs with my own conscience."

In addition John said, in an excess of gratitude, "I will not let you down, Doctor, I swear on my son's life!"

Mary gasped at this and gave John a hard stare. Doctor Love shrugged it off. "You will get the use of the SES for life, Mary. You don't think I mean any harm to Xavier? It is Social Services you have to fear not me. You know the difference between a rottweiler and the SS? You can get your baby back from a rottweiler.

Mary felt she had to laugh at this but the two men went on staring at her until she said, "I swear on my son's life!"

Tilly reflected that "use for life" was a strange term in any contract. Did it mean the life of the Streatham Esoteric Society which could be folded at any moment by the board of trustees, Victor and Jenny? Or the life of John and Mary which was about very finite. And the lifetime contract meant that a massive debt became their lot the minute they went against Victor's will. So although the contract did not mention their first-born son it might as well have.

If John and Mary ever went against the Streatham Esoteric Society, i.e. crossed Victor, their whole debt for the freeloader contract would become due quite legally. They would be bankrupt with impossible debts.

So any attempt to stop Xavier being apprenticed to Victor at the age of seven would be seen as a breach of contract. They did not have to do as Victor said but woe betide them if they did not!

Although there is an old saying, "The Devil looks after his own," You can see that the Devil looked after Victor, or perhaps "Victor looked after Victor" would be a better way of putting it. The Devil did not look after John and Mary at all..

Tilly judged that Xavier was not going to investigate his parents' death any time soon and her background was deep enough to be going on with. She could not resist visiting the fatal night itself but this was a Xavierism. He always wanted to know the facts before anybody else.

She could identify the female character who was with

Doctor Love at the crash site, it was Jenny. The two of them were secretly married as if they intended to adopt Xavier. Nothing was secret from the Mirror of Eternity, Tilly had unique access to any records. Using a trick learnt from Wolf Dietrich von Raitenau, Tilly or Xavier could access any town hall Information Technology system. At that time the only computer in Streatham was in the Town Hall.

Tilly speculated that Mary had resisted Victor's plans. She did not visualise John becoming vertebrate at any stage. This drastic course of action had been the result. She also thought that "drastic" was neither here nor there. For Doctor Love the lives of two acolytes were a small price and easy to pay.

In the event it was one year and three days before Xavier gave in to the inevitable. He had known what Tilly was up to but he professed to be impressed with her research.

It was a dark night but the street lamps were reflected off the snow. John and Mary had borrowed a Ford Cortina from a fellow Satanist. This was all done with Victor's approval. He knew that they were taking

Xavier out of his clutches. He knew they would not get far.

There was a finite chance that the accident would kill Xavier but this was slight. It was unlikely to kill anyone because John was a sensible driver in the snow.

John did not know that the street corner he was coming to was solid ice and he could not know that the steering and brakes would fail. Victor had developed a love for gadgets and he had a device the size of a brick with a single button on it. He pressed the button and the steering and brakes on the Cortina failed. He shoved it into Jenny's capacious handbag so there was no evidence on him. He was prepared to sacrifice anyone. That was how you became a Grand Master.

The car careered off the road and wound up in a ditch. Victor and Jenny took Xavier away from the vehicle and Victor put a tiny device on to the petrol tank.

"We'll tell the little bugger his parents are dead."

"Why are you going to tell him that?" This was a

woman's voice.

"Well they are dead. As good as."

Nice Jenny, the babysitter who had so many games, roughly sedated Xavier.

They were well away when the whole thing went up in a ball of flame. John and Mary were unconscious as they were incinerated.

A fire tender, a police car and an ambulance arrived and Xavier was taken to St Katherine's hospital, The staff wondered at the presence of sedative in his blood. Victor ventured that his parents sedated him for long journeys.

"They ought not to do that." the nurse said crossly.

"It is a bit late to tell them."

"We will have to keep him in overnight Mrs..."

"Love."

"It was very good of you to come here."

"Xavier is like a son to us. I babysit him, though a baby he isn't."

It looked like plain sailing for Victor and Jenny until unaccountably their records got lost and a search found only Victor's dishonourable discharge from the medical profession and a string of convictions for drug dealing.

A couple who had been trying for adoption for some time, Terrence and Geert Hollands, looked a safer bet for young Xavier. Stable relationship. No criminal record. A "good home" according to the social services visitor for whom a good home meant Geert kept the place spotless and it showed a good middle class ambiance.

There were other disappointed would-be adopters in this situation. There always are.

Victor went back to Streatham with his tail between his legs but he never forgot the Hollands family. He aimed to have a terrible revenge on them.

3 If Xavier Ruled the World

One Tuesday night, we were sitting in the living room of Xavier's flat. Tilly was visiting her cousin in Cornwall so it was just the two of us and a bottle of Shiraz.

"What's on the television?" I enquired mildly.

By way of answer, Xavier wiped his hand along the top of the set and looked at his palm. He didn't have to say, "A Handful of Dust." But he said it anyway.

I opened my mouth and realized I didn't need to say anything.

Xavier was not there. Only a handful of dust falling to the chair and my look of open-mouthed astonishment showed he had ever been there at all.

No amount of experience, even experience of Xavier, had prepared me for this. I fell back on my mother's old maxim "Sit down before you fall down."

Within seconds I didn't have to cope with the situation. Xavier had returned. Yet it was a very different Xavier who was sitting, exhausted and bedraggled, in the chair opposite me. What follows is Xavier's version of events. He is an unreliable witness. Half of what he says is improbable. The other half is wildly inaccurate.

There was no transition. From standing by the television he suddenly found himself in a railway compartment. The people around him were talking English or Polish. There were copies of *The Metro* strewn around the place. Clearly he was in London. The train pulled in to Croydon station as if to confirm this.

Some people were standing. There was a weirdie with a beardie (Xavier's phrase) who used his luggage to reserve a seat for his imaginary friend.

Two police officers boarded the train. To his amazement, one of them saluted Xavier and they rounded on the bearded gentlemen.

"There are people standing on this train, sir. You are occupying a seat that you are not sitting in. Agreed."

"What?"

"You are in violation of the Selfishness Act."

There was a look of some surprise somewhere behind the beard.

"In plain English, you're nicked sunshine."

Croydon station is half a mile from home and Xavier thought enough strange things had happened for one day and felt in need of a little lie down.

"Xavier!"

"Barry!"

"Going to the wedding?"

Xavier reflected that none of his friends were teetotal so he could probably get himself a drink or two to help him come to terms with the situation.

"Yes of course, erm."

"Barry?"

"No I remember you, it was the venue."

"Well I am surprised but we are meeting up in Ye Olde Boar if you would care to join us."

Sure enough, after an hour in Ye Olde Boar, Xavier was more relaxed.

The happy couple included an old friend from University, Adam Trevithick, but Xavier could not get a good look at the other side of the aisle from his position in Church.

When the priest reached the vows, Xavier learned the other party was called Steve. The priest raised his hands and said "I now pronounce you husband and...." he frowned briefly and continued, "and husband."

"God bless you both."

"You may kiss the....oh just kiss."

After a boozy reception, Xavier found himself back at the flat in bed and fully clothed.

He drifted into the living room and settled down with a large black coffee and daytime television.

"*Jack, I can't believe a word you say.*" Tracy screamed.

"*Tracy, give me another chance. Marlene means nothing to me.*" Jack shouted.

"*You were in bed with the slag.*" Tracy screamed louder.

"*It wasn't what it looked like. I swear on your mother's grave!*"

"How about a proper conversation?" thought Xavier.

"*Why can't we have a proper conversation?*" Tracy asked mildly.

"*You never give me a chance!*" shouted Jack,

"She is now." Xavier said out loud.

"*Well I am now.*" Tracy agreed. "*We could sit down and discuss it instead of screaming clichés* (she pronounced it clitches) *at each other.*"

Xavier thought, "This will play havoc with the viewing figures."

"*'Together' will be back again tomorrow if it has any viewers left after that outbreak of reasonableness.*" the announcer concurred.

On his way to Ye Olde Boar, Xavier entered a public convenience.

"Scrupulously clean" he muttered.

"So it should be."

The speaker was a cleaner holding a super-mop as if it were a mediaeval weapon.

"Hollands?"

"Mr Pikestaff?"

"Well , Good God man, you have certainly grown. You are spoken of as un grande fromage these days."

"And you are..." Xavier looked round.

"A lavatory cleaner, boy. Call things by their right names."

"Unusual occupation for a head teacher though."

"Well, Hollands, I always told you that you would never amount to anything. I was so certain of it that I placed a substantial bet that you would never amount to anything. I had to mortgage the old school you see. And now you are such a luminary I have lost everything.

"And wipe that silly grin off your face."

"You do seem to have been hoist with your own petard don't you?"

"Pardon?"

"Hoist with your own..."

Two police officers caused Xavier to pause.

"'Did you suggest that this gentleman had been 'hoist with his own petard?'"

"Certainly."

"Prevention of Xenophobia Act. This is a public place."

"Yes."

"You were quoting Shakespeare, Macbeth?"

"Hamlet."

"Don't make things worse for yourself," and the handcuffs were really tight.

"The penalty for quoting Shakespeare in public," Xavier explained back in our own timeline, "was five years in prison. Seemed a lot longer to me."

"Longer? You don't look older."

"Well, it was always the first day of spring."

I raised an eyebrow.

"OK I made that bit up. However, you will admit that there is a timeline in which I rule the world."

He looked sheepish. "Rather draconian wasn't I?"

4 Hospital Prison

Xavier was in prison. There are no surprises there. His lifestyle sailed a bit close to the wind from time to time. The problem was that from this prison there was no escape. He was in hospital, or as his mind put it, the prison hospital wing because of his delusion. His delusion was that he was in prison.

"Do you know where you are, Xavier?"

"Is your nurse's uniform a clue? Hospital is my guess."

"And who is the prime minister?"

"Attlee."

He thought for a moment,

"Attlee, Churchill, Eden, Macmillan, Home, Wilson, Heath, Wilson, Callaghan, Thatcher, Major, Blair, Brown, Cameron."

"My money is on Thatcher. She's dead but she won't lie down."

"How about Cameron?" the nurse asked in all innocence.

Xavier gave her ten minutes on his opinion of Cameron and how in all but name he was a reincarnation of Thatcher.

And the words "bright but deluded" were ticked on his chart once again.

"Jailer, bring me water." he said once.

"You are nil by mouth" came the stern reply.

"So a jailer would bring me water but you won't?"

There was no reply to that but eventually his persistence was rewarded with a damp hexagonal sponge.

His dreams were strange.

A laser was about to make an incision into his brain to remove his delusion.

Xavier, being Xavier, could not resist saying, "You expect me to talk?"

To his surprise he heard the surgeon say, "No Mr Hollands, I expect you to die."

For once he was pleased to be awakened by a blood sugar test.

He did not always welcome these tests. He was unable to take communion as he was "nil by mouth" but he could have a visit from a priest. He was less then pleased to have someone come in and take his blood sugar level in the middle of this very private conversation.

Geert made two visits. On the first one she brought a cake with a file in it. (Confiscated) On the second she brought Arthur Koestler's *Darkness at Noon* (Confiscated. Too depressing).

Tilly was visiting relatives in the north, in uncivilised places without wi-fi or mobile phone coverage. She got one message through to Xavier before she started the long trek home.

"What kind of prison allows wi-fi, smart phones and I believe you are getting on with the coding for Mirror of Eternity? I checked. None do."

This gave Xavier pause for thought but most of all it made him long for Tilly. He would do anything, even lie, to have her back.

"All sentences have a length. How long is mine?" he asked a friendly nurse.

"Sine Die." (without a day being named) was her accurate but unfortunate reply.

For three days he would not talk to anyone. Then Tilly arrived.

She started talking about the coding for Mirror of Eternity. Xavier was a bad programmer and never left comments to show what the program did. Tilly had learnt her bad habits from him. Within minutes he was convinced this was the real Tilly and not some stool-pigeon.

Then she kissed him and he made assurance doubly sure.

"I want you back in my bed." she said simply. He didn't have to agree but he did.

The second thing she did was to bring him his rosary which nobody else had thought of. With it, his tenuous grasp on reality seemed to strengthen.

His sarky answers began to fade away.

As a result he was taken from Intensive Care to a ward.

"I want to go home. Why can't I go home?" was the refrain of one patient. It was a refrain he kept up all night.

Another tried to claim Xavier's bed for his own. He had wandered from the ward and could not identify which of the eight beds was his. The small detail that Xavier was in the bed did not seem to make a difference to him. In the end a nursing auxiliary persuaded him back to bed.

One patient had a visit from his wife and a row with a nurse about being drunk (his wife had brought him a bottle of pop which might have had whisky added) and going home. Then he just got dressed and made a break for freedom. He was never seen again.

It was remarkable how many patients, whatever the illness they suffered, just wanted to escape from the hospital. Just like a prison, Xavier thought.

Then came the day when Xavier faced the usual questions.

"I am in a hospital. Your name is Rose (this was on the Orientation Board) I am in a safe place. I am being well looked after." This too was on the board.

"So you don't think you're in a prison?" asked Rose.

It was on the tip of his tongue to point out that the food would be better there but he decided against. He confined himself to "No."

Doctors had to ask him the same questions and he had to sign forms. And wait. And wait. He made the usual joke about why patients are called patients. In the end it was 24 hours before he was able to go home.

Suddenly, in the privacy of their own bed, Xavier laughed. "We fooled them, Tilly. We fooled the lot of them."

"You mean?"

"Of course. We fooled them that I thought I was in hospital."

Something in the air – Grosvenor Square

Terrence often revisited Grosvenor Square in his memory and reveries. It was the place where a police horse had trodden on his foot but he had many positive memories to balance against that. In his smoke-filled study he remembered the camaraderie, the sense of "something in the air." which had wafted over the channel from France and the sheer electricity of the moment.

In cold retrospect, he could see that while the revolutionaries in France were talking about detailed plans for a new society, they did not have a single one of the old regime in prison. It is all very well to talk about a fairer world but having a few capitalists and bankers in preventive detention tells the world you are serious.

The workers who occupied the factories had the right idea. If you can't imprison the capitalist at least capture his capital. However, this was a long way from Terrence's thoughts at the time. He was intoxicated with a mood, an atmosphere, rather than Jack Daniels.

A giant blue banner bore the words,

"STORM THE REALITY STUDIOS AND RETAKE THE UNIVERSE"

It summed things up for old Terrence. These were people who wanted something different but were not yet sure what.

The march was confined to the left-hand side of the road. A voice yelled, "Up against the wall, motherf******s!" and the police were forced to let the march take over the whole road.

For most people it was their first ever demonstration and Terrence revelled privately in this fact because it was his first time too.

The My Lai massacre in which 340 unarmed civilians were gunned down by the US forces in Vietnam came as a blow to people who usually saw the US as the good guys and the Communists as the bad guys. It was in this state of ambivalence that they joined the demonstration.

The route was a disaster. The police could not allow them to attack the American Embassy and for the Americans it was sovereign territory. Inside the embassy, there was a machine gun pointed at the door in case any got in. This was a hint to the Metropolitan Police that the demonstrators had best not get that far.

Terrence eventually made use of the Mirror of Eternity to visit his heyday and see his young self. However his main purpose was to find a person.

He had spoken often of his friendship with the anti-war activist called Ian May. It had begun on the train up to London for the demo and continued for years afterwards. Ian for example had no illusions in American Imperialism and found the North Vietnamese regime beyond reproach.. He had chapter and verse on American crimes which were a real eye-opener for Terrence.

It was child's play to track down Ian, even among the thousands on the demo but Terrence thoroughly enjoyed his day.

Recently Ian had been in dire straits financially and Terrence was only too glad to help out. Terrence's job title had been Director of Research so he had dispensed with the whole business of research by picking the brightest graduates from each year's crop and retiring to his office with his foul pipe.

This was very lucrative and he was happy to use the money to help an old friend. Xavier and Tilly didn't say yes or no but they were keen to meet this old friend.

Wolf-Dietrich von Raitenau was a wholly remarkable man. For example, he is my friend on Facebook despite the small detail that he has been dead for 400 years. This was as a result of what he dismisses as a"mere conjuring trick" which moves a cursor on a screen. Xavier and Tilly eagerly learnt this "mere conjuring trick" and it opened a whole new world to the Mirror of Eternity. If someone were reading a paper record or a book the observers had to possess their souls with patience.

Electronic records however would succumb to the "mere conjuring trick".

Terrence introduced his old pal Ian to the delights of Ye Olde Boar. All or most leftists like old pubs without widescreen TV. It is the origin of the phrase, "the revolution starts immediately this pub closes!" The two old pals chewed over old times for an hour and shared a bottle or two before Terrence's son and his daughter-in-law arrived. Xavier brought his cane and air of bonhomie,

Although Tilly lived in a world where information was all ones and zeros in cyberspace, she brought a chunky paper file with her which Ian eyed askance.

{I may as well tell you I was invited to block Ian's exit and look menacing. I can block an exit with the best of them but Xavier knew I was rubbish at looking menacing – Narrator)

For a while they chatted about the Vietnam war and the many young Americans who had died. They talked about how the My Lai massacre had shown the world that "Communists" were just human beings not monsters. Tilly sat quiet through this and Ian relaxed.

"I am sure that Grosvenor Square was a turning point in the thinking of a lot of people but some were there with quite different motives, wouldn't you say, George." she said.

A rabbit in the headlights would have a similar expression to that on Ian's face.

"The young lady has made a mistake. My name is Ian and I have been an anti-war activist ..."

"There is no mistake. The Metropolitan Police have been paying you under the name of George Davis and they obligingly add a photograph." Tilly took a sheaf of pay slips from her folder and put them on the table,

Xavier's cane knocked the legs out from under the police spy when he tried to leave.

He produced a police radio. Xavier looked at it in amusement.

"Dead as a dodo?" Xavier asked calmly after George had fiddled with it for a while.

"These are your reports," said Tilly conversationally, "they make interesting reading.. For example, (she shuffled the papers) 'I could seduce GH but it is not worth it. Her political involvement is slight.' and here again, 'I could blackmail TH as his employer would not approve his political activities. Unfortunately three board members also sympathised with the anti-war movement so it might not work.' You then go on to detail your work disrupting non-violent protests. You obviously earned your pay."

"Did you even believe in peace?" This was an agonised Terrence.

A cynical look appeared on George's face. He was pleased in a way to talk without the mask.."Peace!" he spat the word out like an obscenity, "All you want is for the trade unions to run the country and the Commies to run the trade unions. They would walk all over us.

"And American Imperialism?" asked Terrence.

"The Americans are just doing what they have to do to stop the Commies."

"Well thank you George, All you have said, including a recording of that little speech is now being emailed to all the peace groups. You will be no more use to Scotland Yard."

"Silly Girl. I retired ten years ago."

"Well retirement is a trade union concept. I am surprised you went for it."

George was not use to people laughing at him and he left Ye Olde Boar in some confusion.

"Sorry to ruin your dreams, Terrence."

"I have other dreams, Tilly."

And a mere conjuring trick recovered the £1000 Terrence had already paid to George.

Ouija

Xavier downed a swig of Shiraz and started a new conversation.

"You know that the Ouija board has no intrinsic scientific value."

"Like the Mirror of Eternity?" asked Tilly innocently.

Xavier smiled and tried to look as though he had expected this response.

"And yet it can focus the mind of a group for good or evil. For example..."

I could tell Xavier was off on one of his stories but he was interrupted rudely.

"I will have you know that all this talk of Ouija boards is out of order. Ye Olde Boar is an ancient pub with ancient rights. In the courtyard there is still a metal post to which we tie people and burn them if they bring witchcraft in here."

The speaker was Bernard, the new manager of Ye Olde Boar and his struggle with the accounts had not left him in a good mood.

Someone round the table said "How about we adjourn to the Hobgoblin then?"

And before Bernard knew what was going on, his most profitable customers were streaming out of the door and 250 yards down the road to the very inferior Hobgoblin.

Tilly gave him a pitying look as she left.

Around the table in the Hobgoblin with its "Frightened you might taste something, Lagerboy?" beermats, Xavier continued, after he had haggled over a decent bottle of wine.

"I suppose you know why it is called Ouija?"

"Yes and Yes?" I ventured.

"In fact they asked the board what it should be called and it came up with the name. When they asked what that meant, it said 'Good luck!'

"Naturally my parents, Geert and Terrence would have no such nonsense in their house but I went to visit friends from school and we would sit up late at night with cider or light ale and see what the board could tell us."

"Do you believe in ghosts then?" Asked Tom, a newcomer to Xavier's tales of mystery and imagination

'Not then, not now. I do know that the darkness reveals strange shapes. My great aunt, for example, was excited by the tale of the strange man who stood on the street corner watching her as she scurried home in the blackout. It is a better story than the truth the cold light of dawn revealed."

'Which was?' I obligingly asked.

"He was a pillar box."

"So why contact the non-existent spirits?" Tom persisted.

" I was with friends whose spirits were quite enough to set the planchette moving. And they had stories (mainly untrue or half true) about their relatives (as I had of mine), which were great stories and we were having fun. The Ouija was officially forbidden fruit to us and we revelled in it for a time. We had a lot of laughs contacting 'the other side.' "

"It all went very well until I was away for one session. I only arrived late and found that my friends were all in a state of shock.

"Chris, one of my friends, was the only one who seemed capable of any kind of coherent speech. Eventually he told me that their talk to the undead had been hijacked by a forceful character called 'Tiberius'.

"It soon became clear that this 'Tiberius' knew something about each of them around the table and they found the planchette was remorselessly spelling out accusations which they were unable to deny. Some of the apparent conduct of my friends was quite shocking. It included everything from petty theft to random acts of cruelty to (in one case) incest. My first, rather selfish, thought was that I was very pleased I had not been there. My second thought was that I would have thrown the Ouija board on the fire rather than let it ruin our evening.

"Don and Eddie were incoherent. I tried to find out from Chris what drugs they had been taking but he insisted that as far as he knew they had taken no drugs.

It was a cold night at casualty. We vainly hoped our parents would never know what had happened to us. In practice they all turned up at the hospital and the recriminations began then and there.

"We are all grounded and we were forbidden to see each other ever again. Geert caused a small sensation in Croydon by seeking to ban Ouija boards from toy shops.

"If only there were some way of investigating what really happened." said Tilly.

Xavier looked at her. She looked at him.

It wasn't just their mutual attraction which sent them off before closing time to their flat.

"Exact date?" Tilly was businesslike as the drugs needed for the Mirror of Eternity kicked in.

"3 September."

"So anything in late August or early September," said Tilly.

Xavier nodded.

"Let's hunt down Tiberius!" Tilly was in her least saintly mode that night.

The 'prime projection' or 'best guess' was that one of the three, Chris, Don or Eddie, had been Tiberius or that two of them had ganged up on one until it all got a little out of hand. It was to Chris's house that they went because that was where the Ouija experiments had taken place. It was also the only address which Xavier could remember. It was reached through a part of Croydon where the rat-catchers never went. This was not because of the rats but because there were some violent residents. As is the way of Croydon this area was right next to a posh area where Chris's house was to be found.

The route was significant because it led from Chris's House to his local pub. He was under-age for drinking but the enforcement of the law was less stringent then.

When Tilly and Xavier arrived at the house they found why Chris was not en route for the pub. He was lying on the living room floor, the very room where the Ouija experiment had taken place. He was SCREAMING. The neighbours were an incurious group of people or they would have been round to investigate.

Xavier always talked quietly when using the Mirror of Eternity although he could have had a voice like Brian Blessed and made no difference. Those who were being observed could not see or hear the observers.

"I think the neighbours have heard it all before."

"What the hell is it?" asked Tilly, unnerved by the noise.

"Well it sounds like a bad trip. LSD? "

Chris was shouting about the ceiling (nine feet above him and immobile) coming down and crushing him. They could only watch as he gradually brought himself under control and rolled to the doorway (thus avoiding the ceiling) and crawled to the kitchen where he made himself about a litre of vitamin C and tried to drink it down in one go.

He lit a cigarette. It was a self-rolled one and without the benefit of the smell they could not tell if it was tobacco or some other weed. He held it in a shaky hand, let the ash fall where it may and tried to calm himself down.

Both Xavier and Tilly noted the absolutely disgusting state Chris left the kitchen in and decided they were growing into their parents.

"I never left a mess like this." Tilly protested.

"Not that you remember?" Xavier asked wickedly.

"No I mean I... Oh shut up Xavier!"

They walked with Chris down the mean streets that led to the pub. The pub itself was divided into a saloon bar and a public bar. The saloon bar was carpeted and had tables and the public bar was more spit and sawdust. Chris strolled up to the bar and ordered a triple whisky which he downed immediately.

"What is he doing for money?" asked Tilly

"Well he was still at school and didn't have a paper round." Xavier answered

"So his parents indulged him?"

"Perhaps, or perhaps they didn't know they were indulging him. I keep thinking of the accusation of petty theft Tiberius came up with. There had to be something to pin on everyone and it was a small thing for Chris to admit to.

"He had no siblings." he added to rule out the incest accusation.

"Cousins?" asked Tilly

"He might have had. He certainly mentioned an uncle. Norm was a really very embarrassing uncle. Every family has one.

They waited and watched as Chris and the other customers gradually became more drunk. At 10 o'clock, which was close to closing time, there was an unholy rush to the bar. Chris bought two drinks. He would not have been the only person using that ruse to get in more drinking time but the second drink was a lager and lime which was not like Chris at all.

On cue, Don arrived and Chris handed him the lager and lime. To Tilly's surprise, though not to Xavier's, the two embraced like lovers.

"They do it to shock," he explained. "These were the days before gay rights and we were a bit ahead of our time."

Their conversation was mainly about calculus which was a new topic that term and one with which Chris was struggling.

They left together and it was clear they were not going back to Chris's house. They did not speak much on their way through the drizzle to Don's house. Soon they were settled into Don's living room and enjoying a bottle of Don's father's wine. Snuggled on the sofa their talk dwelt on non-calculus topics like sex which is an endless source of fascination for teenage boys or perhaps not just teenage boys. They spent a deal of time on speculation about "what lesbians do" which then drifted into a discussion of feminist politics and then they somehow got to the Ouija Board.

"I believe that the spirits of the dead are all around us and there is a very thin veil to pierce for them to communicate with us." Chris began.

"Well something guides the planchette. It always moves and despite a few spelling errors it manages to make some kind of sense," Don agreed, "It might be the spirits of the dead within us, our memories of our relatives who have died which causes it to move, but we cannot be sure that it is the spirits of the dead who are at work. It could just as easily be the work of evil spirits sent to corrupt us."

"Corrupt you!" Chris shouted gleefully and started tickling Don mercilessly. "I'll corrupt you, the evil spirits will just have to get in the queue."

When they were breathless and ready for another drink, the topic had subsided and no more was said of it that night.

One thing Tilly did notice however was a painting in the hallway,

"Did you notice the painting in the hallway?"

"You mean the picture of Caligula." Xavier said authoritatively.

"Tiberius" said Tilly quietly.

Back at their home, Tilly was enjoying a cup of tea and Xavier was having a last brandy. They both had their smart phones out and they were comparing notes.

"Well it is not too likely that the Tiberius in the picture is involved." Xavier began.

"But the name must have been chosen for a reason."

"His name was a byword for sexual deviance."

"You're making me blush," and he actually was although the cold night and the brandy might have been complicit in this.

"When he died the mob cheered," Tilly continued, "They then fell silent as rumours that he might still be alive alive circulated. When he was confirmed to be deceased they chanted 'Tiberius to the Tiber!' which was where they unhygienically threw the bodies of criminals."

"On the other hand, he was accounted a greater general than Julius Caesar."

"That is not 'on the other hand' by any means." Tilly said, "The ability to kill a lot of people does not transform a man into a saint. In any case, Julius Caesar wrote his own history in which the killing of hundreds of Gallic peasants was represented as a great victory in battle. Apart from the fag of translating his interminable 'Bellum Gallicum', I found that the insufferable self-satisfied arrogance of the man was sickening."

"So are we closer to finding out who OUR Tiberius was?" Xavier wanted to know.

"We haven't even seen Eddie yet so it would be a bit premature. There are only three suspects?" asked Tilly.

"You suspect who? The Ouija board? Spirits from the vasty deeps? Me?"

"Oh definitely you, sexual pervert," said Tilly putting an arm around Xavier and bringing the conversation to a close.

The following night, after a quick reconnaissance of school records and the electoral register, they were able to find Eddie's address. It was a place Xavier had never visited.

"I knew Eddie as a charming young man with a wicked sense of humour."

The scene they walked in on suggested otherwise.

Eddie and his younger sister were in the kitchen at the table. He was doing homework and she was cutting out shapes in paper with a pair of scissors.

Eddie looked up.

"You're going to cut yourself." he said without inflection.

"Not!" She responded spiritedly.

His hand flashed out and caught her wrist before she could withdraw it. The scissors were in his other hand in a second and he had them poised between her right thumb and forefinger, ready to make a deep and bloody cut.

"Yes!" he shouted, adding "I could really hurt you."

The girl started crying.

"Now, now Jessica. You know I was only kidding."

He put the scissors into a drawer and backed his chair against the drawer.

"Nasty scissors. Nasty scissors. All gone away now. Here Eddie kiss it better. You know you have to do what I say!"

He held her hand in a vice-like grip and kissed it tenderly. Then he tickled her and tickled her until she stopped crying and she was helpless and breathless with laughter. Then he abruptly let go of her and returned to his homework as if she were not there.

Eddie's parents arrived.

"So sorry we're late love, we just got gassing with Laurie and Edith and you know how those two like to talk!" Eddie's mother wrapped her arms around him as if she would absorb him. It was perhaps just as well she could not see the mingled contempt and scorn on his face.

"It was so good of you to look after Jessica. I hope she was good and didn't say anything spiteful this time."

"She was not too bad." Eddie conceded.

"Finished your homework have you?" was his father's contribution

"Well I wanted to go round to Xavier's to go over the calculus."

"No he bloody didn't!" said Xavier.

"Well you had best go now." his mother said, "and blame the lateness on us or on Laurie and Edith truth to tell."

Eddie didn't need telling twice and he was out of the door, putting on his raincoat in the hall and banging the front door in less time than it takes to tell.

He walked for what seemed a long time until he came in sight of The Swan. The Swan only had one bar. There was a carpet and small tables.

Eddie's eyes lit up as he spotted a man in a bri-nylon suit, the latest fashion, and strictly Brylcreamed hair. He was seated alone and nursing a pint of brown ale. He paid no attention as Eddie approached.

"Ti..."

A raised hand enjoined silence and made it clear who was in control here. The man took a pull at his pint and said quietly,

"Call me Norm. Call me Norm in here."

"OK. Norm. How are you?"

"More to the point, Eddie, how are you? And how is that little Jezebel of a sister of yours."

"Behaving herself."

"I hope she is behaving herself. You have to make her behave."

With a smile, Norm took out a pair of handcuffs and played with them. He opened them and closed them and looked searchingly at Eddie.

"You would like to use these on her wouldn't you?"

When there was no reply, he lowered his voice, "Are you dying for me to try them out on you, then. Is that it?

"I am just off out the back. Get yourself a drink," Norm put a ten-shilling note on the table, "and meet me in five minutes."

Out the back was a gents' toilet which was presumably absolutely foul. Neither Xavier nor Tilly could tell from their noses. They both knew from their wide experience of pubs.

There was only the light of a distant street-lamp and they had to make out what was going on as best they could.

There was nothing to be seen of Norm. The sudden light from the bar door showed Eddie. Norm was out of the shadows in a second and he was pulling Eddie's arms behind his back. The handcuffs clicked.

"Now for some fun."

Norm put his hand down the front of Eddie's trousers and repeated, "Now for some fun."

"Tiberius," Eddie said.

"Shhhhhh" said Norm and tightened his grip on Eddie's hardening cock.

"A bit of pleasure," he tightened his grip painfully, digging in the nails, "a bit of pain."

Xavier decided he had all the information he needed and went back into the light of the bar. Tilly followed.

It was a sore trial for Xavier to sit in a bar without a drink and nobody to serve him. He thought of the fine bottle of Chilean Merlot at home and was comforted.

"Tiberius?" asked Tilly.

"There may be two, there may be thousands, of Uncle Norms in the world. But my money is on Chris's Uncle Norm widening his interests from young Chris to his school-friends." said Xavier after a while.

"And I think I know his target or targets."

Their next port of call was the Ouija seance itself.

They were keen to complete this investigation so they worked through the night from their perspective.

They sat and watched as the three assembled. The youngsters exchanged greetings, jokes and gossip and then settled down around the table with the Ouija Board.

It was all the normal nonsense until the planchette spelt out,

"I AM TIBERIUS!" and then it began to spell out in the filthiest possible language the masturbatory habits of the four. It included Xavier as if Norm's acolyte were following a script and acting as if unaware that he was not present.

Tiring of this, Tilly went up to Chris's bedroom.

There, ensconced in all his glory, was Norm. He had expensive and large headphones on. His hand was down his trousers and his other hand was holding a Woodbine cigarette.

Occasionally coarse remarks would emerge from him,

"Xavier, I own your pretty little arse." is the only example I am giving here.

In time he realised his mistake when Xavier arrived late.

Xavier came upstairs because he had an aversion to being in the same room as his younger self, similar in intensity to Wolf-Dietrich's dislike of his mausoleum. (He considered the mausoleum tasteless and an unfortunate reminder of his untimely death).

Norm could clearly hear his arrival on the headphones and decided discretion was the better part of valour. He left a packet of Woodbines and four sets of handcuffs behind as he exited by the back door just as the younger Xavier was ringing casualty.

The next day, Tilly noticed that the morning newspaper looked odd. It was a broadsheet and yellowing. It was indeed a copy of the *Croydon Advertiser.*

The front page had a photograph of Geert telling a council official "what for". The lengthy article talked about her campaign to ban Ouija boards.

It was Xavier who drew Tilly's attention to a small article on an inside page.

"Norman Cole, a well-known local character, has been committed to Warlingham Park (a local mental hospital, Xavier explained). While the balance of his mind was disturbed, Mr Cole insisted that he was the Emperor Tiberius and violently assaulted a police officer who begged to differ. He was spared a prison sentence but committed to Warlingham Park indefinitely.

The Dictator and the Clairvoyant

The dictator and the clairvoyant were enjoying a little private time in an underground room. It was furnished comfortably enough and there were no officious Nazis taking notes of the whole conversation.

"There are only two alternatives. Either the British Empire will help us to crush the Bolsheviks or we will crush the British empire with the passive support of the USSR."

The clairvoyant sipped his tea and made a gesture which indicated that he was out of his depth with this discussion. Hitler actually smiled.

"I know my friend, it must seem strange to you that I talk of Churchill as an ally when he is full of "fighting us on the beaches" bluster and bullshit. I can remember when Churchill made speeches supporting Italian fascism and deploring the "bestial appetites and passions of Leninism." The British Royal family have proved to be very amenable to persuasion, especially that Edward, and England has its own Fascist movement. Although to be honest they are a bit foppish and that Mosley is an upper-class twit of the kind we have had to liquidate in large numbers to make Germany strong.

At the mention of Churchill, the clairvoyant became suddenly animated and laid down the astrological charts for Churchill, Stalin and Hitler on the table. As he described the finer points of his analysis, Hitler's expression was unreadable.

All too soon the meeting was over. And Hans Herman discreetly ushered the clairvoyant from the meeting.

"Mein Führer, I trust that was useful."

"Between you and me, so long as British and Russian intelligence know I was consulting a clairvoyant and that we discussed the USSR and Britain that will be enough. They will waste time and money finding out what they think I plan to do by employing their own clairvoyants and as ever I will make up my own mind.

"Send in Menzel." he added.

Menzel was a bad speaker. He looked down at his notes too much and did not look Hitler in the eye. What he had to say, however, was interesting.

"They can fight us on the beaches all they want." He began, "we retain air superiority in numbers and anyone on the beaches will be subject to attack from the air. The concept of Blitzkrieg has not entered into British military thinking. It will not occur to them that we can have paratroops, light armoured cars and motorcycles controlling the streets of London while they are fighting on the beaches.

"As for Churchill and the Royal Family,they will not be 'defending their island' they will be off to Canada. Everyone in the UK will be made aware of this.

"A high proportion of the upper classes will welcome us with open arms so long as we are seen as the enemies of Communism. They can be persuaded to see the pact with Moscow as a temporary expedient. We can confidently schedule a victory celebration through the streets of London for six weeks from today.

The Führer sat for a long time in the underground room. His face was drained of emotion and his thoughts turned inwards. In time he sent for Müller.

Field Marshall Müller was a much better speaker than Menzel. He stood up throughout, he did not consult a single note and he spoke directly to Hitler.

"The Russians as a people are totally racially inferior to the Aryan Race and they cannot fight. They have been further weakened by Communism which does not allow any true leadership to emerge. The pact with Berlin and Moscow has further taken the edge off their aggression They long for peace, they dream of peace and we can give them Blitzkrieg

"Apart from that, we could not hope to kill as many promising Russian army officers as Stalin has already killed for us in his purge last year. He feared they might support Trotsky (who appointed some of them) against him. Compared to Trotsky or Voroshilov, Stalin is a blundering idiot of a General but he will insist on getting his own way.

"Russian armaments have nothing to compare to the Tiger Tank. They will only be able to retreat or die."

He gave another ten minutes of facts and figures before the Führer dismissed him.

The moment of decision came that day as a Mark coin fell to the floor in the underground bunker. It landed heads. The road to Stalingrad and the destruction of the Third Reich had begun.

The Future

"Is it worth looking into the future?" The occasion was a most unusual one, Geert, Terrence, Tilly and Xavier were sitting round a dinner table enjoying a meal with some fine wine and trying to make civilised conversation.

"Well if you use a clairvoyant or Tarot cards you are more than likely to get moonshine, if you use the Mirror of Eternity you will get an accurate answer and that will be worse." Terrence said.

"How so?" asked Xavier, who had heard this argument before. He was not sure the others had.

"You will see a lot of good things in the future, the downfall of the Tories, the expropriation of the 1% but your mind will drag you inexorably to one inevitable fact. Your own death.

"It will be there at your waking, it will be with you when you go to sleep. It will darken your daylight hour and it will haunt your dreams. It is inevitable and you can do nothing to avoid it."

"Well just a cotton-picking minute," Geert loved contradicting Terrence, "If I saw that I was going to be knocked down by a truck on the 3rd of July next year, wouldn't I keep completely off the roads on 3rd of July? So wouldn't I create a little temporal paradox, for the sole purpose of annoying my husband."

"You might bring the truck incident forward in time a little but the fundamentals would remain unchanged." Terrence insisted.

"Or create a parallel universe in which you survive. The universe in which you died would go about its business but the universe in which you survived would have a completely different trajectory." Xavier held by the parallel universe theory which he thought was supported by the writings of Boethius. It wasn't. Plenty of contemporary physicists would hold to his view. So would many contemporary philosophers. Just not Boethius. One day Xavier was going to use his skills to convince Boethius .

"Coffee anybody," said Tilly, rising.

"Surely *Doctor* Hollands has something to say about this," Geert had not lost her catty edge.

"I would go into the future with a specific research project in mind. It would not be to find out about my own death. I would treat the future as I treat the past, a source of data. I do not know whether there are parallel universes. Since they are "parallel" and can never meet I will leave that speculation to those better qualified than myself. Does that answer your question?"

Geert fumed silently.

"Now about that coffee."

Terrence and Geert had to go shortly after that.

"A specific research project?" said Xavier when they were gone.

"I will tell you in the morning. We have more pressing matters" and they embraced.

"It involves going forward in time 200 years to witness the election." Tilly began, "I have done a reconnaissance and it seems that elections to the parliament are annual. First however I think we need to solicit the opinions of Wolf-Dietrich von Raitenau who has a unique perspective on democracy.

Xavier was not sure that Wolf-Dietrich's perspective was needed but he was so pleased at the idea of meeting his old friend again that he held his peace.

The graveyard of St Sebastian was not a welcoming venue at the best of times and Wolf-Dietrich was as vexed as he always was when he had been snatched from a dream of Salome Alt. Still he warmed to the presence of Xavier and Tilly and even agreed to accompany them on this fact-finding mission.

The first fact they picked up was that there was still a Queen of England which Wolf-Dietrich thought only right and proper. In the pictures on the internet however, the Queen looked very young for the job and this gave Tilly an idea. Using a "simple conjuring trick" to access her friend Google Tilly was soon able to ascertain that the Queen of England the previous year had been a different person and the year before yet another. She had about as much power as the Queen of the May, no matter what some folks say.

Buckingham Palace had long since been turned into council flats but one of them was always reserved for the Queen and her family. She was indeed elected on the First of May. Monarchists and Republicans had to like it or lump it. After fifty years they decided they liked it.

Black Rod had been retired and given a stick to play with. There was no summoning of the commons to the Lords.

"Why is that?" Asked Wolf-Dietrich

"They abolished the House of Lords," said Xavier.

Wolf-Dietrich just shook his head at that.

"Have you looked at the moon?" asked Tilly.

They looked. It was a waxing gibbous moon and it was unmistakeable green.

"The green which you can see is a distant relative of wheat adapted to the lunar conditions. Most of it is under glass and will be harvested. There will be 'Luna Pops' on sale in the shops soon although most of the harvest will go to feed the 50,000-strong population of lunatics.

"That is a childish and insulting term." Wolf-Dietrich began.

"Except that they apply it to themselves. They have reclaimed it." Tilly insisted. "The rest of the wheat you can see is trying to survive in the lunar atmosphere and contributing to the terraforming of the moon. It will be OK for humans to live on the surface in another hundred years."

"Now about the election we are here to observe." Wolf-Dietrich was keen to keep his companions on track.

"There are no news channels. They were continually being disproved on social media so 80 years ago a woman known only as 'Alice' developed an application which could create a bot..." Tilly began

"a bot is..."Xavier interrupted

"I know what a bot is." said Wolf-Dietrich, somewhat surprisingly

"Anyway this bot will filter the facts for you according to your own predilections. You can choose 'no celebrities' or 'no sport' and you can filter still further. I have chosen to focus on this election but there is surprisingly little coverage."

After a pause to let this sink in, Tilly added,"This is because there are no political parties."

"They were abolished?" asked Wolf-Dietrich with altogether too much relish.

"No they more-or-less withered away. There were no careers to be made in politics. The ten MPs only get the average wage of a skilled worker – no expenses. And they can only stand once. Next year a different ten take their place.

"And what do they do?"

"They all boast their ability in Mathematics or Statistics. The real decisions are taken by the general public who can promulgate and then vote on propositions. They verify the proposals. Or negate them of course.

"For example?" Wolf-Dietrich asked.

It was Xavier who answered. "They rejected a proposal to limit the number of whales killed in the North Sea."

"Mind you," added Tilly, "that was only because it contradicted a recent motion to ban whale fishing altogether which had a larger vote.".

"So all you have told me is this. You have abolished the monarchy and replaced it with a show. You have scrapped the House of Lords and replaced it with nothing. And these ten men..." Wolf-Dietrich thundered.

"Six of them are women" Tilly interrupted.

"These ten people are just a rubber stamp for the will of the people? You have effectively abolished the state. Where is the chance for a strong leader to emerge in all this mess?"

"Like the Dictator?" Tilly said innocently.

"Well the Dictator was a special case and he required special measures." Wolf-Dietrich said defensively.

"You have analysed the situation and concluded that there is no way for autocracy to gain the upper hand?" asked Tilly quietly.

"You could say that," Sensing a trap, Wolf-Dietrich answered cautiously.

"What about a military coup?" asked Xavier.

Wolf-Dietrich's eyes lit up but Tilly had done her homework on this too.

"There was a public inquiry in which it came out that there were more admirals than battleships and more generals than tanks..."

"What are tanks?"

Tilly brought up some pictures and Wolf-Dietrich was fascinated for half an hour with the potential of this battlefield weapon. Although he was an Archbishop, his earliest ambition had been for a military career. Now he briefly imagined himself driving the Bavarians back with a division of tanks.

"Most of the officers were pensioned off. You can still read their blogs complaining that the army is no career for a gentleman these days. And their main complaint is that the officers are now elected for a fixed term and then have to serve in the ranks."

"That is utterly ludicrous. Officers require specialised skills."

"And it is from the people with specialised skills that the officers are elected. Regiments regularly send NCOs for training and the officer class is no longer recruited from the 'Hooray Henries'. So the chances of a coup are greatly reduced."

From the Diary of Wolf-Dietrich von Raitenau

I will be pleased to get back to the old certainties of my life in Salzburg. It was good to spend time with my young friends but the world they showed me seemed horrific. Rank and file soldiers are not fit to take decisions and the common people are not fit to frame referendum questions.

Of course Tilly is right in saying that they are better educated and better informed than at any time in history and I must put my faith in that. "Blessed are the poor" but being blessed and the recipients of charity is one thing. Putting power in their hands is another!

Robinson report

The following story can only be found in an encrypted email in a forgotten account. It is not on Xavier's system and nor are any of his case notes.

Xavier reasoned that the state has the resources to find and verify it if they want to. He is very certain that there are things the security services would rather not know. His attitude has softened towards MI5 since he realised they wanted him to stay alive. Although they could not use the Mirror of Eternity themselves (and indeed they had experts to verify that it should not work, despite the demonstrable fact that it did) they still felt it might have some use for them in the future. So his hostility to a group of people who spy on trade unionists and peace campaigners and produce dossiers of lies for Government had mellowed...but only slightly.

A job covering six months for an undisclosed client had involved detailed surveillance of the Robinson children and the theft of one of their toys.

Although nobody can actually detect the use of the Mirror of Eternity, Children are very aware of a sense of "being watched" so it was often from some distance that Xavier and Tilly watched the young Robinsons.

They always played with each other. If there was another child, a Smith or a Jones or a Patel, Xavier's background check always showed that it was a Smith-Robinson, Jones-Robinson or Patel-Robinson.

In 1840 Jack Robinson had robbed his first shop. He went in with gun. He asked nicely for the day's takings. He shot the shopkeeper in the shoulder because he felt he was delaying matters and made off with £3 and 19 shillings.

The Rozzers had him bang to rights and he went to chokey for a 20 stretch (or in English he went to prison for twenty years).

In prison however, Jack Robinson, ever the villain, found there was more than one way to profit from crime.

Somehow or other (*to be honest I am fairly certain how it was done - Narrator*) Jack managed to father four children by three different mothers while he was in prison. He had obviously done favours for guards who in turn did favours for him.

And it is on those favours and on those children that the astonishing prosperity of the Robinson criminal fraternity was founded.

Jack seldom left his house in Mile End Road. He seemed to lead a charmed life. He got other people to carry out his robberies and they were successful. His rivals seemed to be having a bad time of it.

His children naturally used to play in the neighbourhood. And it was at this time they developed the most remarkable toys.

They made their own. On the outside they were nothing special, lead soldiers gave way to cars which were superseded with Star Wars figures as the years progressed. The children played with them all day and when Xavier was able to steal one in the twentieth century he made an interesting discovery.

The children said very little to each other that was not connected with the game so his surveillance using the Mirror of Eternity was not useful. Nor was there anything in the Robinson household to arouse suspicion.

The toy was a Millennium Falcon. The detail was perfect and the finish looked professional. He put it on the work bench in order to examine it. It took about five minutes to assemble the tools to take it apart.

"I was very lucky to get this. Young Robinson had a collision with another child as I was passing and I was able to grab this and bring it here.

"Will you look at that. It is overheating!"

When he was in a position to dismantle the toy it had scorched the workbench and there was nothing inside but fused metal.

At the same time there was an encrypted package intercepted by his security network.

It took Xavier, who relished decryption,the best part of 25 hours to decrypt the message. It was as follows:

"I was very lucky to get this. Young Robinson had a collision with another child as I was passing and I was able to grab this and bring it here.

"Will you look at that. It is overheating!"

As soon as he had this information, Xavier erased all the data on the Robinsons from his systems. He took a USB to the local library, logged in with a fake ID and uploaded the encrypted information as anonymously as possible. He then over-wrote the whole of the USB with information about Ibiza.

Twenty minutes later, Tilly opened the door.

"Vice Squad, madam, we have an order to confiscate all the computer equipment on these premises."

With extreme politeness and consideration, the police took away every device in the house including mobile phones. Xavier was to deliver his phone to the station as soon as he got home.

Xavier seemed unconcerned when he got home.

"Vice Squad? They are looking for child porn. They will not find any. They may plant some but their more savvy technicians will realise there are two mirrors of this system and if they have no child porn on the mirrors then they have a lot of explaining to do."

There is no such thing as a secure location when it comes to state surveillance so Tilly and Xavier had to make use of the Mirror of Eternity to go back to a time when the state had less interest in the thoughts of its citizens.

In 1984 Orwell talks about his protagonists going where "the trees were too thin to contain microphones." Now a leaf could contain a thousand microphones.

In a run-down 1930s cafe, where they had no intention of eating anyway, they compared notes.

Tilly began,

"The Robinsons found out early on that informing on other criminals is more secure source of income than committing crimes themselves. They continued to commit crimes on a credible scale but we can only conclude the police turned a blind eye.

"The demographic analysis overlaid with crime statistics show that the Robinson family is established in over 100 locations now and most are in crime black spots."

Initially the children just engaged in earwigging in the streets. Now the methods are more sophisticated to say the least."

"Moreover," Xavier added, "notice how clean the Robinson households were of any surveillance equipment. The information from the junior spies must go direct to a police command centre.

"We will decline the contract to investigate the Robinsons. My guess is that it comes from the security services themselves. They just wanted to know what we could find out.

"We stonewall them. We found out nothing. We know nothing."

"Isn't that rather cowardly?" asked Tilly quietly.

"The trick is to pick your battles. We cannot win this one. You don't mind being married to a live coward rather than a dead hero?"

By way of answer, Tilly gave Xavier a kiss which he returned with interest.

The Seeds of Time

"Can you look into the seeds of time and say which grain will prosper and which will not?" The questioner was Bernard, the new landlord of Ye Olde Boar. Xavier and his coterie had soon tired of the Hobgoblin and gravitated back to Ye Olde Boar despite Bernard's half-jovial threat to have Xavier burnt at the stake.

"Well it's 'grow' not prosper and I remember you wanted no witchcraft nigh Ye Olde Boar."

"Look Xavier, I am sorry about all that. I had been struggling with the accounts. Tilly has lent me a hand since and I won't mention the W word again."

"Except," he added after a moment's thought, "this doesn't involve any black magic does it?"

"Who knows what it involves? The less you know about the Mirror of Eternity the better if you want my opinion. Only an adept of the left-hand path can truly control it."

Tilly laughed and said, "Oh do behave, Xavier, Bernard has put a proposition to you, a paying proposition. We don't want to turn away business. Nor will I have the program I have been coding with you wrapped up in a lot of mumbo jumbo. There is no adept of the left-hand path, whatever that is, required to work the Mirror of Eternity."

Bernard had stopped listening at the words "paying proposition" and it took a while to persuade him to continue.

"Well what I want is some information about the solar system. For example; will there be a manned landing on Mars? Will we go back to the moon? That kind of thing. I want to impress the Astronomy Circle with my precognition."

Well naturally Xavier wanted to know all about the Astronomy Circle and when it met before he continued. He had got an honorary membership out of Bernard before he would proceed any further.

The meeting of the Astronomy Circle was on the following Wednesday. They were all over Xavier because he was the first new member they had had in ten years. He got to see and touch their 10 inch reflector telescope. Bernard was more than a little miffed because he had had to wait a month for that privilege.

It was not enough for Xavier to know if there was to be a nicely alliterative manned mission to Mars (it took place in 2053); he also wanted to tag along.

The mission was a European Space Agency venture going from Cuba. For the take-off the two men (Jacques and Corin) and women (Berta and Andrea) were wearing the latest in space suits and bracing themselves for the tremendous acceleration that was still necessary to get into space. They were only going to the space station where they could get on board the Mars mission vehicle.

They traversed the short corridor in the space station using hand-holds. They were still wearing the bulky space suits and moved clumsily. They had to go in single file. Naturally they did not notice Xavier.

It was going to be a long boring journey to Mars and Xavier was only going to stay with them for part of the way. He intended to skip to the approach to Mars after a day or so on the space ship. The Euronauts (as they were called) were not going to be travelling in suspended animation so the whole voyage would be 28 weeks. They did have recorded terrestrial television in three languages to ease the tedium. They had magnetic chess, backgammon and Ludo and for a period at least they could Skype their families on Earth.

Although the Euronauts were German, French and English, they had adopted English as their chosen language (much to Xavier's relief). Their reason was not Xavier's convenience but the convenience of the Americans. Although the ESA were nominally in charge of the mission, the equipment was largely made in the USA or China and they needed to liaise with the US and China during the mission. China's space agency also used American English as a language of convenience.

The most stunning feature of the Mars probe was a result of developments in Information Technology for which Xavier had been partly responsible along with hundreds of others. The crew could, at will, make the skin of the craft appear transparent. They could look out at the stars with a clarity which was unobtainable on Earth and they could also magnify constellations which were of interest to them. Weirdly they could then label the stars in different colours and trace lines through space.

Xavier watched fascinated as they did this. There was enough information here for Bernard to wow the Astronomy Circle for weeks on end. The most interesting finding for him was the number of earth-like planets which had been discovered. There were planets in the so-called "Goldilocks Zone" - not too hot and not too cold – which could therefore, in the view of scientists on earth, sustain Earth-like life.

Unsurprisingly the Euronauts of the Mars mission were fascinated with these planets and their possible life forms because those planets could be their next port of call. Mars did not sustain life, well not as we know it. Although there was water there, the planet was way outside the Goldilocks Zone so the scientists on Earth had reluctantly concluded there could be no life there, despite the canals. They had decided the canals were an optical illusion.

For a moment, Xavier's thoughts turned to his own form of life. He, the 'real' Xavier, was safe and sound in his apartment in London but he was most definitely also in space with the Euronauts. He knew that he would easily survive outside the space craft and he imagined that he could manage the freezing cold deserts of Mars. So was he a form of life? And were there other similar forms of life undetectable to Earth science on the planet itself? And if so where did they originate? Where was their 'London flat" situated.?

If the putative forms of life on the Goldilocks planets wanted to explore our solar system then perhaps some version of the Mirror of Eternity would be their best way to explore it. His fertile imagination made another leap. When he went on these Mirror of Eternity missions with Tilly he could see and hear her easily. This opened up the exciting prospect of seeing and hearing the other explorers of Mars when he got there. And learning their language? Well perhaps they had the forethought to learn the languages of Earth. Or they had the universal translator of Science Fiction. A third possibility would be that they had a mind-reading capacity which rendered a universal translator unnecessary.

Or, a still small voice in his head said, the whole thing was a figment of his imagination. Yes that seemed the most likely case.

Xavier's Martian expedition

Xavier took the precaution of not actually landing with the landing craft but on the surface of the planet to observe the arrival. In fact there were two arrivals. First the spacecraft landed and Jacques, Corin, Berta and Andrea emerged. They immediately started assembling their rugged base camp.

The alien, when she arrived, was something of a disappointment. She didn't look alien. She looked as if she came from Earth. In fact her first words to Xavier confirmed this.

"Are you another tourist?"

"Yes I am from Earth." Xavier responded, "My name is Xavier Hollands."

"What? Surely not the Xavier Hollands?" was her gratifying response. "You are the stuff of legend where I come from. My name is Zamida by the way and the planet we colonised was rather unimaginatively named Tellus.

"Some people on old Earth had known for some time that the nuclear war was coming. By then space travel had become commonplace and they formed an organisation. After Isaac Asimov they called it "The Foundation" but it could just as well have been called "Armageddon out of here" to quote one of Xavier's – well one of your – old jokes.

"Some people wanted to use a space craft to convey two of every animal but they were overruled by the majority who wanted to get as wide a range of humans on the ships as possible. In the end there were eight ships which took off from Earth over the next five years. Our ancestors had to be ready for space flight and there was an ethnic monitoring policy to make sure there was the same racial mix on Tellus as there was on Earth.

"The generation which landed on Tellus was not the generation which had left the Earth. They had been educated in the history of the Foundation and with the mission to save the human race. They had also gained every scrap of knowledge about Tellus that was available.

As we approached the planet which was to be our home, we gave thanks for the pioneers that had landed on Mars and begun the exploration of other planets, Jacques, Corin, Berta and Andrea. The same people who are setting up their doomed base camp over there."

"Doomed?"

"Perhaps I shouldn't have said that. However the legends said nothing about your trip here and Xavierology is a distinct branch of history on Tellus. On Tellus our scientists and technologists read of The Mirror of Eternity and after many setbacks and disappointments they were able to reproduce your work. Was there really a school called Ye Olde Boar where you instructed your students and treated them to wine?"

"Well it was a pub and rather hope Tellus has pubs." Judging by the blank look on Zamida's face the answer was no. "It was a place where friends could gather and enjoy good company and alcohol in equal measure and where I shared my stories with anyone who was interested in listening. It was where I met Tilly, Doctor Tilly Hollands, who had a key role in writing the coding of The Mirror of Eternity.

"That is great news. Our experts concur that Tilly was a figment of your imagination because you were homosexual."

"Well I hope Tellus is ready for the news that I was bisexual and, after I married Tilly, heterosexual. She is the co-author of the Mirror of Eternity program as it eventually developed."

"Not Terrence Hollands?"

"To my father goes the crown for the initial idea but he never had any faith in the eventual development of the Mirror of Eternity because it was unscientific."

"At the time the flight of the bumble bee was unscientific because it did not obey the rules of aerodynamics." put in Zamida.

"Exactly. So my father did not endorse the Mirror of Eternity although he eventually had to concede that it did work. Tilly saw it as an interface between dream and reality, legend and history. It was in fact a link between parallel universes of course."

"Our scientists are still puzzling over what it is. They only know that it works."

"Is this a private conversation or can I join in?" Xavier had refrained from jumping out of his skin when Zamida arrived, his response to the newcomer showed equal sang froid.

"Hello, my name is Xavier and this is Zamida."

"Mine is Krystal. Are you named after..."

"I was named at the same time as **the** Xavier Hollands."

"And Zamida, what is the year from your point of view?"

"It is 150."

"How interesting. I am from 200, fifty years after your time."

"I can do the Maths," said Zamida with a sweet smile intended to take the sting out of her remark.

"Perhaps the most important information I can give you is that Tellus is not alone. We have radio signals from other colonies. It is probable the radio waves took up to 200 years to reach us. We have been broadcasting since your day and before so there may eventually be a reply to us from them.

"One of the other colonies is actually called 'Planet America' and they welcomed all comers like the words on the Statue of Liberty, 'Give me your tired, your poor, Your huddled masses yearning to breathe free, The wretched refuse of your teeming shore. Send these, the homeless, tempest-tossed to me, I lift my lamp beside the golden door!'"

"The original USA didn't stand by those words." said Xavier.

"Well these people seem – or at least so they tell us- to have shrugged off their trumpery. They seem to be genuinely trying to be the democracy America once had the chance to become. That's what they say. We only have their radio broadcasts to go by."

"Did they say how they left the Earth?"

"They were quite open about that. A flotilla of small ships left from all over the Earth in the very midst of the nuclear war. Not all of them survived the trip to Planet America. Some were destroyed on the ground or in the air by surface-to-air missiles as they tried to escape. They were seen as traitors by the world powers who used the full weight of the mass media to blacken the reputation of any dissidents; anyone who opposed the war. This was true regardless of which side of the war they were on. The world was gripped by a war psychosis and people had to conform or else. The same rule applied in those regimes which called themselves democratic.

"Curiously, we have information that the same world powers had their own plans to create a colony on another planet but we have no information about what happened to them."

Krystal and Zamida broke off their conversation to look at the four Euronauts. The disaster came quickly. The four were still in space suits and half way through constructing their base camp.

The sky darkened suddenly. Although the atmosphere of Mars is a fraction of the atmosphere of Earth nevertheless the dust storms of Mars were terrible to behold. It did not destroy the space camp. It could not unseat or destroy the spacecraft. What it could do was destroy 90 percent of the water supply in a tank which Jacques, Corin and Berta were manoeuvring from the spacecraft. Andrea was working on the camp. The three were blinded by the dust which developed an electrostatic cling and the wind did the rest. Andrea rushed to help. It is very hard to rush in a spacesuit and the reduced Martian gravity. It did not take them long to realise that they were, in Zamida's expressive word, "doomed".

The three travellers from afar could do nothing to help them. That did not stop them discussing the matter.

"As you should know," Krystal was addressing Xavier, who she now accepted as the creator of the Mirror of Eternity, "we can observe the past, or in your case the future, but we cannot influence the outcome. It would create too many 'Xavier paradoxes' as they are known to us. You could send a message back in time to switch off the machine which sent the message. Paradox."

"Or two parallel universes in one of which the machine sent the signal and the other in which it did not."

"That parallel universe nonsense is so ridiculous," Krystal said, "it isn't even wrong. It is unprovable one way or another which makes it literally absurd."

"So we just watch them die?"

"We witness the heroic first attempt at interplanetary travel. There will be others, we know that, and they all lead inexorably to Tellus, to the survival of the human race. I have no intention of watching the heroes die, I have an appointment to keep."

And with that, Krystal returned to her own time. With a rather longer leave-taking so did Zamida.

Xavier moved himself forward in time but by the time he had realised he couldn't even give the heroes a decent burial he knew it was time to go back and write up his report.

"Well this will do nicely." Bernard said, when next Xavier visited Ye Olde Boar, "All these Goldilocks planets and their dates of discovery are fascinating. It is a pity you don't have more about the Mars landing but you can't have everything.

"I suppose you won't need to come to the Astronomy Circle any more will you, Xavier?"

Xavier weighed his options and eventually decided on a "no" and another bottle of Cabernet Sauvignon.

"Now can you imagine a planet where there are no pubs?" he asked the table at large.

Visit to Tellus

It was inevitable that Xavier and Tilly would use the Mirror of Eternity to visit the post-nuclear-war colony of surviving humans on Tellus but the invitation came in a rather unusual way.

They were investigating a murder. They were uniquely placed to do this. The Mirror of Eternity could show them the murder itself. It could give them the identity of the murderer and then they could trace him back to his home. Xavier insisted on calling him "light-fingered Larry" throughout. He said that somehow a murder viewed through the Mirror of Eternity seemed less real and he also argued that the police must develop a detached attitude to crime because they have to deal with it day in and day out.

"A Policeman's lot is not a nappy one," sang Tilly, "but come off it, Xavier , you don't even like the police."

"Maybe not. I didn't like them much when they are beating up miners on Thatcher's orders. This is murder, though. I may dislike the police. I dislike murderers more."

Xavier and Tilly sent a text with all the details of the crime to a police friend of Xavier. It may seem odd that Xavier had friends in the police force but he was just naturally friendly and anyone who turned up at Ye Olde Boar became his friend.

So when Inspector John Johnson turned up and took Xavier aside to solicit his services he was only too happy to help. Tilly was only too happy to tell Inspector Johnson their scale of fees.

"I don't believe in the Mirror of Eternity." The Inspector said.

"The fee remains the same though, whether you believe or disbelieve. Just go by the results." Tilly said. There was to be no haggling about this.

It was while they were following the murderer home that they realised they had been joined by a third person.

"Tilly, this is Zamida. Zamida, this is..."

"I am delighted to finally meet you, Tilly. And we now have the opportunity to set the record straight on your role in our history. I have come to invite the pair of you to visit Tellus in my own time, 150. It is very important for all women on Tellus that we establish the role played by Tilly in the programming of the Mirror of Eternity. The program code is written in the same enigmatic way, without any comments to show what the code is about. At the moment our Xavierologists are convinced that Xavier did it all on his own and..." she lowered her voice, "he was a homosexual."

"There is no need to lower your voice. Nobody but us can hear you for one thing and homosexuality is quite legal in the 21st Century. I think your timelines need refreshing a little. It was illegal in the 1950s, not now." said Xavier.

"We will need the co-ordinates – the International Celestial Reference Frame – of the planet at the moment in time you would like to see us and we can be there at any time of your choice. There is no charge." Tilly added the last point for effect. It didn't have any.

To Xavier she just said "Xavierologists?"

"It's a branch of history on Tellus."

"And woefully inaccurate to boot." said Tilly dismissively. "And remember that this is the planet with no pubs. How are you, how are we, supposed to manage?"

"No pubs does not mean no alcohol. How can a human community exist without any alcohol at all? I doubt if they have had time to cultivate the grape on this planet however "Goldilocks" it might be, but there are many ways of making alcohol." Xavier said.

"Fermented milk, potato peelings, yak dung?" Tilly said helpfully.

"Well they probably don't have many yaks there. They eschewed the whole idea of having two of every animal if you remember. And if you drank a fermentation of yak dung and did not know what it was it might taste like nectar of the gods. Especially after the first and second glass."

"Anyway," he added sadly, "we probably will be unable to eat or drink there unless Zamida knows something we don't."

Zamida who had been listening to this exchange with an amused smile, had to shake her head at this. She gave the ICRF numbers to Tilly as if she had memorised them. In fact most of the inhabitants of Tellus had computer Implants. These implants were rather more powerful than 1,024 laptops and it had not been hard to get the requisite information.

They deliberately arrived early for their appointment with Zamida so they would have time to do some sightseeing. The town was one of fifteen on Tellus, according to Zamida. It was surrounded by fields. They seemed to be growing Earth crops where they could but there were some which were clearly indigenous to the planet. The planet was particularly rich in fruit and great orchards of fruit trees and bushes were patrolled by watchful robots waiting for them to ripen and catching any windfalls before they touched the ground.

"So they are an agrarian people. That sounds peaceful." said Tilly.

"Yes. Although all the crops are monitored by computers and hand-picked by robots, they are still farmers of a sort. The town obviously supports other occupations – teachers, doctors, scientists"

"Xavierologists." Tilly interrupted.

"Yes, Xavierologists that you are about to prove wrong. That is what I would like to see."

They wandered through the streets of the town to Zamida's office. The streets were scrupulously clean. The street lighting, which was just coming on, was more than adequate and they could see the homes and gardens which made up most of the town itself. The homes appeared to be gleaming clean and all the population had incredibly tidy gardens. The few people that they saw could not see them.

When they reached Zamida's office she was ready with a conference call to the major Xavierologists. They were apparently present in the room although Zamida assured them that they were in various places in the town and in other towns. There was no capital city on Tellus and intellectual activities were widely distributed. Each town would have had its own Xavierologist for example. She proved her point by playfully waving her hand through one Xavierologist who was proven to be a 3D projection which was remarkably lifelike.

The assembled Xavierologists questioned Tilly closely on the function of various parts of the coding of the Mirror of Eternity. Whether those parts were Xavier's or her own, she was able to explain how they related to the program and what they did.

"There were many blind alleys in the writing of the program and many parts of it were dumped. My coding and Xavier's in roughly equal measure." She looked at Xavier and he nodded.

They then turned to Xavier's sex life which was a whole subdivision of Xavierology. Fortunately he had shared all this information with Tilly so there were no nasty surprises for her. He was not remotely embarrassed by any part of it. Indeed the more salacious, the more he seemed to relish it.

Sitting in Zamida's office, looking as if butter wouldn't melt in his mouth, Xavier was enjoying the cross-examination altogether too much in Tilly's view.

The final decision, Zamida forced it to a vote, was that the Xavierologists agreed to give Tilly equal prominence in the history of the writing of the Mirror of Eternity program in future. They raised their hands in the traditional manner and of the 22 present, 17 were for,

3 were against and 2 abstained

"Would it be in order for us to discuss with the five dissenters after the meeting?" Xavier asked. This was a break with procedure and all the Tellurians seemed to find such unconventional behaviour difficult to understand but eventually out of politeness they agreed.

Xavier did most of the talking and he was not gentle with them. It was clearly hard for the Xavierologists, perhaps for all the Tellurians, to have a serious debate. Disagreement was not regarded as proper behaviour. All five went away saying that they would 'think about the points Xavier had raised'. Xavier reminded them that they were in a minority and most of their colleagues had accepted that the conventional wisdom needed to be revised.

Xavier suggested that he and Tilly should go for a walk and Zamida said she had some work to do so she would join them later.

"The Tellurians have something holding back their humanity." Xavier began when they were out of earshot.

"What do you mean."

"The bright houses and beautiful gardens were a clue. There was no individuality to them."

"They were probably cleaned by robot cleaners and gardened by robot gardeners."

"Cyborgs." said Xavier.

"How do you mean?"

"The Tellurians all have computer implants. The computers are very powerful and can out-argue a human brain easily. It would seem as if the tail was wagging the dog."

"The implants are controlling the humans? Yet Zamida seems human enough; playful even."

"Zamida is my source of hope. I think there are humans on Tellus who can master their implants and live a more human life. I want to share this insight with Zamida and see what she thinks."

They didn't have long to wait. Whatever work Zamida had to complete, it didn't take long.

"Tell me about the drugs?"

"I beg your pardon?"

"Sorry if I was abrupt. I am interested. Using the Mirror of Eternity usually requires the use of some drugs which are banned on Earth. I wondered how you managed with that."

"We have no banned drugs here. Anyone who has a drug problem is treated by doctors and the drugs are only supplied by doctors or nurses. As for the drugs needed by the Mirror of Eternity, your hallucinogenics, they are manufactured to the highest standard for those who need them. Use of the Mirror of Eternity is a privilege reserved for scientists and other researchers."

"I think they have another effect. I couldn't help but notice that the other Tellurians are what we would probably call uptight."

"Well, Xavier, perhaps the fact that alcohol is also a restricted drug has something to do with it."

"So if we had treated the Xavierologists to a glass or two of Cabernet Sauvignon they would have been more easygoing?"

"Well I have only read of Cabernet Sauvignon and seen videos but I imagine that would be the case." Zamida was smiling.

Although Tilly had used the Mirror of Eternity to create a hard astral projection she nevertheless dismissed the whole procedure as "mumbo jumbo". She little realised (or chose not to think about the fact) that most serious scientists also dismissed the Mirror of Eternity as "mumbo jumbo."

"Zamida...." Xavier began.

"Not on your Nelly!" said Tilly vehemently.

"I was just about to suggest..."

"I know fine well what you were about to suggest and it is not going to happen. I trust you implicitly of course and I trust you too," she addressed Zamida, "but the thought of my husband naked in a pentacle with, excuse me, a beautiful young woman is one I will not put up with."

"Ah," said Zamida excitedly, "you are talking about the mythical hard astral projection are you not? I have made a study of this mythology and the folklore and of course I find it totally unscientific, like a lot of Xavier's (and Tilly's) ingenious ideas. I am prepared to give it a go. I will of course have no companion with me if that is Tilly's wish."

"There is one thing I have found out, if any of this mythology is true."

Xavier and Tilly looked at her expectantly.

"Well it is simply the problem Xavier encountered in carrying objects, even clothing, into the dreamscape. It is quite a simple matter but only if you know how. And only if the whole thing works at all." Xavier had a sneaking suspicion that she had been reading his mind but that was...

"Impossible?" said Zamida sweetly.

"You were just thinking that it was impossible for me to read your mind. One of the many thing my computer implant does is to enable a rough approximation of the thoughts of others. I trust my approximation was accurate.

"Now you two must show me how to draw this pentacle. We do not have candles here but the scented oil-burning lamps we use in our homes will just have to do. I must warn you that my first act will be to visit all the Xavierologists at the meeting today to tell them there is something else they have gotten wrong."

Zamida was grinning and positively bouncing with excitement. She took them to a spare room next to her office. She had to resume her real-life persona to deal with removing the lumber which had accumulated there over time. She cleaned the floor to Xavier's exacting instructions and brought the Mirror of Eternity console into the room. She used a kind of magic marker to draw the pentacle, distributed the aromatic oil lamps and sprinkled holy water around the pentacle in a circle.

The others retired to her office and she closed and locked the door. Ideally her real self and her astral projection should not meet.

Zamida took about an hour to shake up the Xavierologists. She appeared as a vague mist in the middle of her office which rapidly resolved itself into a solid figure in purple and gold, wearing what Tilly deduced was the latest fashion in Tellus. Zamida turned round so they could admire them.

Somewhat to their surprise, she stripped them off and gave them to Tilly.

"They are real. I didn't dream them up. One of our fashion designers did that. I just borrowed them from his atelier. We don't make a thing about nudity here by the way so you have no need to blush, either of you."

Zamida repeated the form of words which enabled her to manipulate physical objects. She then took them to the designer's atelier to demonstrate.

A few days later, Xavier returned to Tellus. He directly accessed Zamida's office. He took with him a crate of the finest Chilean Cabernet Sauvignon.

"Now you just need to invite a few friends round to try something new and you will start the process of undermining the hold the implants have on the behaviour of Tellurians. It is not their fault. They think in the way computers think but there is more to humans than logic. You know that as well as anyone."

"Goodbye Xavier. Should I say 'au revoir'?"

"Mais oui." Xavier departed with a smile.

The impossible co-ordinates

Tilly's insistence on attending next time Xavier went to a rendezvous with the Tellurian Zamida had something to do with curiosity and something to do with Zamida's insistence that Tellurians 'did not make a fuss about nudity.' She trusted Xavier implicitly of course.

In the event, Xavier got Tilly to carry a crate of wine so Zamida's growing circle of friends was to be treated to a mixture of Cabernet Sauvignon, Merlot and Shiraz. Zamida's friends had formed the impression that Chile was the only remaining wine-producing nation on Earth. There they were victims of Xavier's taste. Zavier's taste often depended on whatever the Co-op had on offer that week.

"I think I have some news for you. Although the news is puzzling." Zamida began. Xavier and Tilly could hardly have any news because to the Tellurians they were fossils from the distant past of their pre-history on the almost-forgotten planet Earth. In the year 150 not only were there no survivors of Earth but indeed the colonists who arrived at their unimaginatively named planet were not the original crew from earth but their descendants.

Only historians would be interested in any news from Xavier and Tilly and many of them were in a huff because Tilly had upset their view of the past. It didn't make them any happier when Zamida had rubbed salt in the wound by creating a hard astral projection – an entity Xavierologists had long dismissed as superstition.

"Our scientists have located the source of the broadcasts from the colony known only as America but the planet it would seem to emanate from is one which is not remotely in the Goldilocks Zone. It is too close to the star which it orbits and it is far too small. You may remember the minor planet Pluto. It was in your era that it was demoted from being a full planet. Mickey Mouse must have been livid."

Tilly and Xavier were so thrown by Zamida making a joke that they failed to laugh. After a pause she continued, "However, we are going to use the Mirror of Eternity here on Tellus to investigate safely."

"A hard astral projection has never used the Mirror of Eternity. In effect we are using it twice. Once on Earth and once on Tellus. It could be dangerous."

Zamida started making what they eventually realised were chicken clucking noises. For someone who had never seen a chicken in real life they were fair enough. At least Tilly had the good manners to laugh.

"Will it be said of the great Xavier Hollands that he was frightened of anything?"

"No but the Mathematics..."

"Screw the Mathematics. Are you up for this? Are you a man or a moose?" Zamida said with glee.

"It's mouse not moose, except North of the Border. But I will of course give it a try now you have explained the scientific basis of your argument with the aid of animal noises and clichés."

"INTRUDER IN SECTOR NINE!" was how they were greeted on their arrival on the planet. This was ridiculous since they were the intruders and they knew they had arrived. As for sector nine..."

"Friend or foe?" was the laughable query from the heavily-armed robot who had been sent to greet them.

"You can see us!" was all Xavier could think of to say.

"I would hardly be pointing a bloody gun at you if I couldn't see you, dumbass."

"Didn't Asimov include something about not swearing in the laws of robotics?"

"No he didn't. And we are not programmed never to harm a human being either. You can see that from the fact I am pointing a bloody gun at you."

There was a pause and the robot added, "dumbass."

"Now if you can see your way to answering a simple question before I destroy you, that would be nice. Friend or foe?"

"We are on a peaceful mission to find out about America."

"You mean you are spies."

"We are on a peaceful mission. We mean you no harm. Surely spies would find out your secrets in order to harm you, dumbass." was Zamida's contribution to the discussion.

The robot did not seem to hear Zamida so Xavier repeated what she had said.

The robot almost smiled, if robots can smile, when one of his prisoners threw "dumbass" back at him but he then continued.

"You are illegal immigrants then and the penalty for that is death."

"Whatever happened to 'Give me your tired, your poor, Your huddled masses yearning to breathe free, The wretched refuse of your teeming shore. Send these, the homeless, tempest-tossed to me, I lift my lamp beside the golden door!'?" asked Tilly.

"Well we got rid of all that when we got rid of the humans."

This caused all three of them to pause. The old nightmare of the robots taking over had finally happened.

The robot made a noise which approximated to laughter.

"The looks on your faces. You think we killed them all? No no no. We just took over and removed them from power. They live on reservations like the aboriginal Americans on Earth. You will probably end up there if the decision goes that way."

"And who takes the decision?"

"Well it takes about ten minutes. We take it between us. You probably call it democratic. I should warn you that the death penalty takes a long time to kill you."

"What do you mean?"

"Well humans die. We don't. So we just leave them to live their lives and then that kills them."

"This planet is far too small to sustain human life and too near to the star it is orbiting." said Tilly.

"Well that is simple. Humans never lived on the surface. There was an extensive cave system within the planet and the Americans really were "huddled masses" for a while within the cave system. Then they used us to extend and extend it until the planet actually has a liveable surface area greater than Earth ever had and most of it consists of spacious tunnels such as this one. The enormous heat of the sun on the surface is used to provide electricity, hot water and heating."

"What about food and oxygen?"

"Sorry your ten minutes are up and I will have to carry out your sentence."

Looking at the disappointment on Tilly's face, he added, "hydroponics and recycling. Now let's get on."

He took them down one vast corridor after another as if showing off the wonders of Planet America to them.

There were iron gates and robot guards at the entrance to the human reservation XXXI where they had been assigned. They had also been assigned married quarters in the reservation. Robot guards accompanied them.

"What about me? Am I supposed to be your second wife?" said Zamida.

"Did you notice that the robot only talked to us?" Xavier asked.

"What about it. I thought he was just being rude."

"Oh no," said Tilly, catching on, "I think he couldn't see or hear you. Which is par for the course for the Mirror of Eternity."

"But," said Zamida, also catching on, "if a hard astral projection goes through the Mirror of Eternity twice then it remains a hard astral projection. Perhaps Xavier could dispense with all the mumbo jumbo and lying naked in pentacles if he just used the Mirror of Eternity twice."

"Perhaps on two different planets. Perhaps the 'mumbo jumbo' as you put it is still necessary but you have encouraged me to experiment."

"Meanwhile," said Tilly, "the fact they cannot detect your presence could be useful to our peaceful fact-finding mission, don't you think?"

"You want me to eavesdrop?" Zamida seemed shocked.

"Exactly."

"Shall I start with the neighbours?"

"OK."

Zamida took her work seriously and spent 12 hours with the neighbours. Tilly and Xavier also went to town and tried to get into conversation with the other residents. They were happy to talk about the new residents but any discussion of Planet America and the robot takeover was apparently forbidden. Whenever Xavier and Tilly mentioned the matter people would look around as if they could detect the listeners by eye.

Zamida came up with a theory.

"I think the whole area is covered by microphone and camera surveillance. Robots do not tire and can keep tabs on the whole reservation night and day. The humans are not allowed to talk about the robots. "

Zamida agreed, "People get 'disappeared' and it is likely that talking about the robots would be one reason for this. Nobody knows what happens to them."

"The robots are completely autocratic, your Wolf-Dietrich would love them." said Tilly,

"No he would regard a mechanical device which imitates a human as a blasphemy and in doing so he would anticipate the very danger which has occurred here. The annihilation of the human race." Xavier replied.

"Not quite." said Zamida quietly.

They waited for her to continue.

"You see human beings can reproduce. In fact I have been wondering why you two haven't gotten around to it as yet."

"The robots didn't sterilise them?" asked Tilly.

"No. They might be autocratic, indeed they are, but behind their 'exterminate the humans' rhetoric there are the echoes of their human designers, they have a sense of humour of sorts, albeit a cruel one, they did not disintegrate the humans but allowed them to live out their normal span and most crucially they allowed them to reproduce."

"We have seen no children here."said Xavier.

"The children are taken off to school."

"And has anyone seen this school?"

"Yes. I know you have your suspicions but the robots found out that human teachers were – much to their chagrin – better than robots, although they couldn't see why. The pastoral staff and the cleaners are all robots but the teaching staff are all human."

"Well I am sure I could stand in as a teacher." said Xavier.

Zamida actually laughed.

When she brought herself under control she just said, "Your 21st century knowledge would not suffice to educate these children," and then laughed some more.

"Moreover the teachers would be under even tighter surveillance than the rest of the humans on this planet." said Tilly.

"Well our ability to read minds, human minds anyway, should bypass the surveillance unless it is impossibly sophisticated."said Xavier.

"And the fact they cannot detect anything I say could be a problem for them. They must think you are addressing your imaginary friend." said Zamida

"Do you know that America used the language of the Navaho Indians as a code during the war." was Xavier's apparently irrelevant remark while his mind transmitted one word to Tilly

"ACKSLANGBA."

Tilly, like anyone who has been to school in London, was familiar with backslang. *(For the benefit of any readers who have not benefited from a London education, it consists of taking the first letter from a word, like B putting it on the end and then adding an A. I have spared you from any further examples in this book – Narrator).*

The first thing which Tilly said (in backslang) was, "It is a cypher not a code so the robots will be able to break it quite easily."

Xavier replied, "It is probably too simple for them. They will be trying to find a language and it isn't one."

They explained backslang, in writing, to Zamida and Zamida soon picked it up. Far into the night they discussed the situation on Planet America and what they could do about it

Rather to their surprise they were visited the following morning by a robot "just to see that they were settling in OK." He conducted the whole conversation in backslang.

"Well they obviously saw through the trick but I think they have revealed their Achilles' heel. They couldn't resist showing off. They could have eavesdropped on us with impunity but they had to let us know that they knew we were using backslang."

One of the things the robot had told them about was the community centre. Xavier went down to find a well-equipped building which catered to the various tastes of the community. The one thing he noticed was that there was no History Club. He promptly put up a card advertising the initial meeting of the History Club for the following night and he booked a room at the Community Centre for the meeting.

Tilly had said that the weakness of backslang was that it was a cipher not a code. The History Club was Xavier's answer. He intended to use it to create a code of his own making.

The History Club

Xavier, Tilly and Zamida waited at the community centre and at first it seemed they would be the only people at the History Club. Then they started to arrive. In the end Tilly counted 110. Xavier had to request a bigger room and a microphone. Fortunately there were no charges at the community centre.

Half an hour talk and half an hour of questions was the format he had chosen for the meeting.

"Tonight I will start off with the English Civil War."

Tilly and Zamida spotted likely members of the audience and Tilly showed them a card. "We are not discussing the robots." They had to take their chances on whether the people they spoke to were stool-pigeons.

On their side was the arrogance of the robots who would be unable to resist showing off their cleverness.

Fortunately Cromwell had the habit of expressing himself clearly. While the Parliamentary Army fought under the confused slogan, "For King and Parliament." Cromwell used the following phrase: "I will not cozen you by perplexed expressions in my commission about fighting for King and Parliament. If the King chanced to be in the body of the enemy, I would as soon discharge my pistol upon him as upon any private man; and if your conscience will not let you do the like, I advise you not to enlist yourselves under me."

Xavier quoted this with some relish. The question session, which extended beyond the half hour and had the caretaker fuming, was very interesting.

It included many of those who had been shown the cards and it was clear from their conversation that they had understood the simple code. Xavier hoped it was confusing to the robots who, he assumed, were unused to analogies. Time and again they returned to the fact that the King had all the arms and power on his side while the Parliamentary Army had no weapons.

Xavier was no Cromwell and he did not have a ready answer to this. He did invite them to the next History Club where they could develop some of these ideas with a discussion of the French revolution. They seemed eager to come.

They waited for some indication that the robots had understood the History Club but it was not forthcoming. One of his problems was that revolutions had relied on bringing the rank and file soldiers over to the people. That seemed unlikely with the robots.

"Unlikely but not impossible." said Tilly.

At the next meeting there were at least 200. Xavier began with a joke so old only Tilly recognised it, "The first rule of History Club is that you do talk about History Club. I am pleased to have so many people here tonight. The format will be half an hour talk and half an hour questions. However if there are any questions left over from our last meeting I will take them now."

A man rose up in the middle of the room.

"Xavier, I think most of us would rather continue our discussion from last time. In particular about the Levellers."

"OK. Well as you know," Xavier began, then he realised that half of them would not know.

"The New Model Army had elected officers called 'Adjutators' from which we get the word "Agitator". Elected officers served Cromwell well during the civil war but they had a political program which went far beyond anything Cromwell envisaged. As long as wealthy landowners like himself were in power he was satisfied. The Levellers proposed annual parliaments, an extension of the franchise, freedom of religion and equality under the law."

"The American constitution?" asked one woman in the audience.

"Well, yes. The American constitution, as amended, contains more specific rights but it is apparent that the Levellers were moving in that direction before they were smashed by Cromwell at Burford."

"How were they defeated?"

"By treachery and by brute force. There was one man, for instance, who posed as a Leveller but was actually a hireling of Cromwell, Cornet Dene, who urged the Levellers to repent of their sinful mutiny in the Church at Burford."

"It was a hard thing for the footsoldiers of Cromwell to find they had only exchanged one set of masters for another." said one of the audience to the general agreement of the others.

Xavier arranged to see this man, whose name was Simon, after the meeting. They kept their conversation to the English Civil War while it was obvious that Simon was talking about the difficulties of making a change to Planet America. The people did not have an army of any model, nor arms. They could see no future in appealing to the better nature of their overlords because as far as they knew they didn't have one.

Tilly said one thing at the end of the conversation.

"It was a pity that the Levellers didn't have a chance to fraternise with the Ironsides, Cromwell's loyal cavalry."

Xavier waited until they were alone, although he knew this was unnecessary, before aiming the thought at Tilly, "Ironsides?"

She replied, "I know the robots are probably something else."

"Titanium."

"Yes well Cromwell's cavalry were not called Titaniumsides and our questioner, who I think is a leading member of the resistance by the way, would probably sort out my subtle code. They must fraternise with the robots more. They have regarded them as inhuman oppressors but we know they have human strengths like a sense of humour (or sorts) and human weaknesses like the desire to show off. A desire you are not immune from yourself."

Xavier went on to a discussion about whether they should have sex in the dreamscape or not to which Tilly just replied, "You can wait and enjoy it all the more when we are Earthside!"

"So tomorrow we try sleeping with the enemy?" Xavier said.

"Fraternising. I know some robots are equipped for sex but I am giving you a big fat NO on that issue. And don't describe it as research either." Tilly was all too wise to Xavier. Try living with a telepath and see how you feel.

Simon from the History Club and Tilly and Xavier were the first to approach the guards on the gates of Reservation 31. They tried all sorts of conversational gambits and were politely rebuffed.

Then Simon started talking about History and the guards were hooked. They knew little of human history and they were all too keen to find out more.

Simon had obviously read a lot and could take them through the stages of human development on Earth. Xavier was more than a little ashamed because his understanding of human development was primitive at the side of Simon's. Simon's understanding of pre-history was quite different from Xavier's and probably based on years, actually centuries, of research. He was glad he had not volunteered to teach and had kept his History Club to subjects he knew quite thoroughly.

Robots never need to sleep although Simon did. Xavier took up the story with the seventeenth century. He was relatively OK with this and fielded any questions about non-European history with the suggestion that Simon would be able to explain that much better than he could.

When he touched on literature, the robots were immediately enthused.

He plunged into the way literature reflected the life of the time through fictional stories.

"How does that work?"

The robots did not have names, I could tell you this one was 40D/487 if that helps.

"Writers make up stories."

"You mean they are lies."

"Lies are intended to deceive. These are not intended to deceive. Stories 'hold the mirror up to nature' but they do not pretend that what they are saying is literally true."

"That still sounds like lies to me."

"There was a girl called Goldilocks who visited the house of the three bears."

"Bears never lived in houses." the robot responded.

"So you can tell at once that the story is not true. It is for entertainment. In this case the entertainment of children."

"Wouldn't the children believe they were true? Especially when they were told them by a trusted adult."

"Yes. To start with, I grant you, they probably do. Then they start to make up stories of their own and realise the difference between 'made up' and real life."

"And adults read these stories too?"

"Well they read the children's stories to children and the adult stories to themselves. And of course there are films and TV stories too."

"And they all 'hold the mirror up to nature'?"

"They give us new ways of looking at the reality of the world. There are well-written stories and badly-written ones. The well-written ones will make us think about the world around us."

The following day, the robot at the gate asked Simon a question. There was no need to pass the information on to the other robots because whatever one knew, they all knew.

"Can you tell me about Shakespeare's history plays because they do not seek to 'hold the mirror up to nature'. They are in fact not true, Macbeth in particular is a fabrication which suited James 1."

"I will tell you all about that but I want something from you. Let my people go."

Simon did not believe in long drawn-out negotiations. He thought it best to get straight to the point.

"That is a quote from Moses, addressed to the Egyptians. Your situation is not like theirs. You are not enslaved. We have just left you on your reservation to die of old age when the time comes. And you cannot inflict us with seven plagues."

"I am not threatening you in any way. Tell me you will consider my proposal."

"There is no proposal."

"Give the humans the run of the planet, let them off the reservations. In return for considering that and coming up with a compromise which everybody likes, we will teach you more about History. You can join History Club."

The robot considered for a microsecond and said "Yes. Now let's get on."

Simon explained that Macbeth with its witches and predictions was a fantasy. It served James 1 but it had entertained audiences for centuries since who had no vested interest in justifying Malcolm Canmore's reign or proving Banquo innocent.

"And," he concluded, "who couldn't be entertained by 'Burnham Wood removing to Dunsinane" when it was really English soldiers carrying foliage?"

"OK. Now about Hamlet..."

It was clearly going to be a while before the robots came to a decision.

All the robots were identical but ultraviolet light revealed the number 40D/487 on the shoulder of the one who turned up to the next meeting of History Club. At the end of the meeting, he stood up and announced, "The humans at Reservation 31 are to be given limited freedom to roam Planet America on a trial basis. If the trial is successful, this will be extended to all other reservations and a renegotiation of human/robot relations will follow. "

"I am sorry, Simon it was the best I could do." he added.

"And one final thing. Xavier and Tilly and their imaginary friend are going to disappear. Now. Simon has achieved the best deal he could get and we will tolerate no more disruption of our authoritarian, autocratic ways."

He looked hard at Xavier and Tilly until, recognising the truth of his statement, they obliged.

They arrived back on Tellus as expected.

"Well that looks like another triumph we can chalk up to Xavier." said Zamida.

"You mean Tilly had the idea and Simon carried it out. I was more of a spectator. Who would have thought Simon would have such an encyclopedic knowledge of Shakespeare's plays."

"I think you will find he was one of the teachers at the school as well as being the leader of the resistance. He was a man only too happy to find a non-violent solution. Robots and humans had to find a way of living together." said Tilly

"And," said Zamida, "he didn't treat the robots as masters or servants. By treating them as humans he humanised them. Changing the subject, did you notice the sky?"

"What about it?"

"When you looked at the night sky it seemed perfectly natural to see stars but the planet itself was entirely underground. The stars were projected onto the ceilings of the vast chambers inside and they were the stars as seen from Earth."

"How did you know that?"

"A little computer implant told me. The sky of Planet America itself was dominated by the equivalent of a sun. The robots had decided that humans would prefer their ancestral night sky. That convinced me they would not try violence against the humans on their planet." said Zamida.

"Well you were right." said Xavier

"However, you would like me to return to Planet America to check on their progress. In a year perhaps?" said Zamida.

"How did you know that was what I was thinking? Oh that computer implant again."

"We must be making tracks."

Seeing the puzzled look on Zamida's face he suggested she consult her computer implant about phrases meaning 'leave'.

She tried to smile at that. Her smile was more genuine when they both promised to return regularly with more wine.

Tellurian

Zamida, like all Tellurians, had a computer implant which provided her with an extension of her mental abilities and in particular her memory. She had in her possession all of the history of Tellus and the home planet of Earth. She was pleased to see that the history of Xavier and Tilly had been corrected and the section on hard astral projections had been modified.

She had started to teach her computer jokes. She started off with some of the worst jokes in existence. She got them from Xavier. Then she got the computer to generate its own jokes. It came up with "Seven days without sex make one weak" and then rather spoilt it by spelling out the word weak in case there was any misunderstanding. It was a work in progress.

Taking a leaf out of Xavier's book, Zamida had set up a history club. This meant that she had to use the facilities provided by her computer implant, which she called Jessica, to get discussion points for the club.

The people who had first had the idea of Tellus were heroes of a sort. They had rescued the human race from the impending nuclear war and they had kept the memory of Earth alive in the children. They told stories of old Earth and its peoples to the children.

Computer implants were commonplace when the rebels left earth but they were all controlled by the state. They would only contain information which the state wanted its citizens to know. The rebels had been, to use a dated term, hackers. They had found sophisticated ways to bypass the state control of computer implants.

One purpose of state control was for the government to have a rough idea of what its citizens were thinking. The rebels had found a way to send perfectly innocent and patriotic thoughts to the state in place of their plans to flee the planet and what they really thought of their leaders which was far from complimentary.

She felt very strongly that a new rebellion was necessary. This was not because the implants were deliberately enforcing conformity. It was just that they did not think as humans did. In fact there was a school of thought which held that they did not think at all. Zamida had not shared this thought with Jessica because it did not seem polite.

The first meeting of History Club was attended by twenty people. It dealt with the rebels on Earth and their use of hacking skills to subvert the government's computer implants.

"These are different from the implants we have?" asked one member, her name was Ruthena.

"Well, Ruthena, the thing is we do not have the hacking skills of our ancestors. So we do not know the answer to that question." was Zamida's careful reply.

"How would we ever get access to those skills." Ruthena persisted. She seemed interested in the topic and Zamida made a mental note to see her after the meeting. The mental note was made using her computer implant. That is how closely human and computer were integrated on Tellus. It could not have been the case on Earth. The rebels would never have been able to hack the implants if they had been that closely integrated with them.

Zamida then went on, in the last fifteen minutes of the meeting, to introduce the Mirror of Eternity. She referred to Xavier as an expert on hacking although she did not know this to be true, Xavier was given to exaggerating everything. That included his own abilities.

Most of the attendees were quite happy for Zamida to do any research. The dangerous hallucinogenic drugs involved in the use of the Mirror of Eternity were enough to put most of them off.

Zamida was encouraged that Ruthena was not put off and was prepared to learn from the Mirror of Eternity. She called it "a perfect tool for an historian." This was most pleasing to Zamida because it showed a mind not controlled by the dull conformity which she observed more and more since meeting Xavier.

Over a glass of Shiraz, Ruthena and Zamida discussed their forthcoming trip and what they hoped to gain in knowledge as a result. It was likely that a long trip would be needed to acquire the hacking skills Zamida was aiming at. She patiently explained to Ruthena that a long trip could be accomplished in a short time through the Mirror of Eternity.

Then Ruthena asked her a question she had never considered, "Why?"

Zamida fumbled around with words for a while before admitting frankly that she did not know. She would however make a guess.

"The Mirror of Eternity gives access to a different reality. Time moves differently there. In a dream, days or months can pass between going to sleep and waking. The Mirror of Eternity is a bit like that I suppose. Certainly Tilly would say so. In your dreams you can go anywhere and anywhen. Science rules out time travel after all and yet that is exactly what you and I are going to do."

By way of response, Ruthena hugged Zamida and they set a date for their adventure.

Through the Mirror we go

The first place Ruthena and Zamida visited was a space craft. It was designed to look as much like an airliner as possible but the passengers showed signs of weightlessness. Their hair was not subject to gravity for example. There were no sense of movement as the powerful engines too the craft to the as-yet-unnamed planet of Tellus. The clocks showed the date and the time on Earth. A separate clock showed the supposed time on Tellus. The dates would not start until the colonists arrived.

The two looked at the faces of the passengers. These were one of the fifteen groups of colonists who had started the fifteen towns of Tellus. One of them was immediately recognisable to anyone who had seen the video footage of the rebellion. There were videos of state broadcasts in the run-up to the nuclear war and this man was the man who did most of them, the Minister of Defence.

"The state relied entirely on the implants to obtain information and they had sacked their internal security personnel." Zamida explained, "The rebels used infiltration. One of their most successful infiltrators was a highly-placed spy. He eventually became the Minister of Defence and was able to monitor the activities of the state. Meanwhile the state continued to believe the fake information the rebels were giving them. If anyone queried it, they had the Minister of Defence to answer to."

"The place from which the spacecraft was to be launched was a closely guarded secret. Not all of the rebels were able to make it. The Minister of Defence only made it by the skin of his teeth."

"Pardon?" said Ruthena

"Oh it's a Xavierism. I think it means he only made it just in time. Others were not so lucky. They died along with billions of others in the nuclear war. The war was sold to the public as a defensive strike, Broadcasts said, 'We will not use the bomb first but we have to be ready in case our enemies use it. We will not be aggressors, we will only retaliate.

"The Minister of Defence was able to leak to the rebels the obvious truth that this was nonsense. If they did not use their missiles first they would be destroyed on the ground. The enemy, in this case Russia, was only using the same logic when they launched their strikes. The remaining rebels sent a message."

"They were praying for us. The nuclear war had begun and the experts anticipated that the whole human race would ultimately be killed by the disruption and radiation. The lack of water, food and electricity meant there was minimal medical care and diseases would probably kill more than radiation. And the nuclear winter would put paid to the rest. A phrase from the time was 'the survivors will envy the dead.'" said Ruthena, "I remember that from History class."

"And the human race was saved by our ancestors," said Zamida, "They couldn't save the millions. They could not stop the crazy politicians but they could save enough to start a new life on Tellus. Next we will visit the rebels. Their secret base did not need to remain a secret and we have exact co-ordinates."

…

"You heartless bitch!" The words were out of Zamida's mouth and there was no way of biting them back. Ruthena just looked at her.

It had not been a good day. The co-ordinates, the secret co-ordinates of the rebel's ship, were wrong. Ruthena and Zamida had wound up in a town street. It was clearly England but it was clearly not the place from which the ship had launched.

They gravitated to a cafe. On reflection, Zamida realised that this had been Ruthena's idea but she had been so devoid of ideas herself at the time that it did not register.

There were two women of a certain age sharing a bottle of wine. One of them put an automatic pistol on the table.

"You're taking a risk with that, Sarah," her companion warned.

"Not in here I'm not. There is nobody I don't trust. I think everybody knows that it is illegal to carry a gun or even a knife these days. It is suicidal not to though, isn't it? And I am not carrying that great thing around in my knickers all day am I, Jane?"

"You should get a handbag. I've told you before."

"And I've told you before that the last two I got was nicked by some low-life in the street. I won't have that again, thank you very much."

At this point the lights in the cafe went out. Nobody seemed unduly bothered and the cafe owner had candles handy to light up the darkness.

"Another bloody power-cut. I swear they are getting more frequent. That is the third today. And they go on for longer."

"Well, Jane, I keep telling you the whole country is going to the dogs. There are queues for everything from matches to cigarettes in the shops. You daren't go out of doors for fear of some ne'er do well attacking you for the clothes you stand up in and another thing..."

Zamida and Ruthena never found out what the other thing was. Zamida had noticed something.

"That man, the one with the black hair, he has been looking at me. He can see me, Ruthena and nobody should be able to do that."

"I was wondering when you would notice Scott. I don't know about you but I am going with Scott to the rebel ship. He diverted us here so that he and I could go together."

Ruthena beckoned to Scott who came to join them.

"You think you are the only one who can use the Mirror of Eternity. Zamida isn't it? You are not. The Mirror of Eternity was known on Earth as you must know. I am going to use it to stop the ship from ever taking off."

"You can't. I mean it is impossible. You can't influence events in history. Think of the paradoxes."

"The people who are paying me, paying me a lot of money by the way, don't care about the paradoxes. And the fact I cannot influence history through the Mirror of Eternity will not stop me making a phone call to call down an air-strike after Ruthena and I have checked out the co-ordinates."

Zamida looked helplessly at Ruthena and then the "bitch" phrase escaped her lips.

Ruthena just smiled and took Scott's hand. The pair of them disappeared.

Zamida tuned in again to Sarah and Jane's discussion. They talked about the weather and swapped gossip about people they both knew. Society around them was crumbling with crime on the streets, queues for everything and power cuts. They were just weeks away from the nuclear holocaust but they did their best to keep each other's spirits up.

She did not know what put the idea into her head, apart from her liking for Tilly (and,she admitted to herself, Xavier). She decided that she would not wait for the usual wine delivery but she would drop in on her benefactors at some time when they were using the Mirror of Eternity. She caught them at a time when they were researching the Robinson family. She explained to them exactly what she had done: Ruthena's treachery and the mysterious Scott who had the power to divert her from her trajectory.

"No." said Tilly.

"No?"

"You cannot prevent the nuclear war. You are thinking of Sarah and Jane. You cannot save their lives. It is a hard truth. The most you could do would be to delay the holocaust and possibly even make it worse, if that is possible."

"In which case...." Zamida persisted.

"You have to stop Scott and Ruthena from sabotaging the ship. That ship and the others are the only hope for the human race. They do not stop the war, they flee it"

"Any chance of help?"

"Of course." said Tilly and silenced Xavier with a look.

"How do I find the co-ordinates, though. They were wrong."

"The prime projection is that you had the right co-ordinates and you were diverted. So if we use the same co-ordinates again and you are not diverted we will get to your target." said Xavier.

"Prime projection?" said Zamida with a smile.

"He means best guess." said Tilly.

"Then why doesn't he say so?" said Xavier, forestalling his critics.

Xavier (Zamida noticed that it was always Xavier) put in the co-ordinates and the three of them were transported to the strangest rebel base they could have imagined.

It was on an island and most of those present appeared to be holidaymakers. There was a bar on the beach. There were golden sands. The tide went out with a slick of sun-cream.

What made it seem less idyllic was the fact that there were armed guards everywhere. The other anomaly was the massive runway which seemed to take up most of the island.

"Is that for the interstellar flight?" asked Zamida.

"Well you know more about it than we do but if it looked like an airliner it probably took off like one too. It would have used conventional engines until it got high enough to leave the earth's atmosphere." said Xavier.

"And the armed guards?" asked Zamida.

"Not everyone here is a rebel. When it became time for take-off (and I am guessing that it is quite soon) then the real holidaymakers would need to be deterred from joining in. Although armed guards seem a bit excessive they would also be needed to deal with any government agents sent to sabotage their efforts."

"We have a unique advantage over these guards. We will be able to see Ruthena and Scott and the guards will not." Xavier said.

"What do we do when we find them? We can't shoot them." said Tilly.

By way of answer, Xavier punched Tilly lightly on the arm.

"Ow! Ah I see what you mean. We can physically attack them. I will admit physical force is not my strong point."

"Well it isn't mine. I prefer trickery: taking your opponent unawares or attacking him or her from behind. They will not expect to see Zamida and they do not know who we are so we have the advantage over them there."

A search of the beaches did not find Ruthena in a bikini or Scott in Speedos so they took to investigating the hotels.

There were three hotels on the island and their unique vantage point let them go from room to room like so many ghosts. Some of the things they saw they quickly tried to forget. When they rendezvoused by the pool they had each drawn a blank. They could detect neither hide nor hair of Ruthena and Scott. They searched the airport and the ship to no avail.

"Well this means either that they have already come and gone, in which case an air-strike is imminent or they have not yet arrived in which case we can still forestall them if we detect them in time." said Zamida.

"We need to detect them when and where they materialise though. What would be the most likely place?" asked Tilly.

After a bit of discussion they decided that the ship itself was the most likely place. The loading of supplies for interstellar flight had almost completed. The trio wanted to urge the rebels to bring the flight forward. Zamida came up with a complicated plot which involved Tilly writing a letter in the 21st Century which would be delivered on this day to warn of the air-strike.

Tilly tried to be patient with this suggestion but there were few ways of explaining why it would not work which did not sound sarcastic. In the end she settled for, "The post is slow but not that slow. And..." She held up her hand to quieten her companions, "there is no reason why they should believe the letter. They could just dismiss me as a crank. Thirdly giving the address of this place to the state would not be a good move. Writing a letter would be a quick way to do that."

Zamida subsided into thought. Xavier and Tilly had gone over the contradictions and limitations of the Mirror of Eternity many times during the programming so they were fairly certain there was no way of influencing the events they were observing.

Zamida was the first to spot Scott and Ruthena. With a cry of rage which probably ruined the element of surprise she ran towards Ruthena and brought her down with an impressive rugby tackle.

Tilly and Xavier tackled Scott. Two against one seemed good odds and they were not playing by the Marquess of Queensberry rules. They had Scott on the ground and Xavier was about to choke the living daylights out of him when he disappeared. A cry from Zamida told them that Ruthena had done the same.

"So what do we do now?" a breathless Zamida asked.

"We wait." said Xavier.

"And we think." added Tilly.

"I should get back to Tellus to tell them what Ruthena has done."

"I think we wait and watch so that you can report exactly what Ruthena has done."

And wait they did. Eight hours later the first missile strikes on the airport arrived. The buildings were destroyed and the runway was cratered beyond repair. The next targets were the hotels. The trio witnessed the carnage as the holidaymakers were slaughtered.

It was only an hour beforehand that they had watched and cheered as the ship which carried "the founding mothers" as Zamida called them had embarked on its long flight.

Ruthena never returned to Tellus. Zamida discussed this with Tilly when the next wine run arrived.

"As far as Ruthena was concerned, Tellus would never have existed in its present form and she wanted to stay with Scott."

"And face a nuclear war?"

Tilly nodded.

"That's insane!"

"I think we have to accept that both Scott and Ruthena were quite mad."

"Well," said Zamida raising a glass of Malbec, "I have recorded her abject failure but we are still no closer to gaining the hacking skills to tame..." and she gestured towards her computer implant.

"We have been thinking about that. We may be able to help."

There are very few things which Xavier will admit he cannot do. Hacking has always been one of them. What he could do, however, was contact a group of very advanced hackers "somewhere in cyberspace" who condescended to answer his questions.

At first they did not believe in the powerful computer implants he was talking about. Then they all wanted one. Then he had to explain that he could only contact someone with one using the Mirror of Eternity. They did not believe in the Mirror of Eternity. So in the end he arranged a face-to-face meeting with Zamida.

The result of the meeting was that they agreed to make the computer implant less conformist and authoritarian but they insisted that one of their members should have one. Xavier said this was not possible. Zamida said she could probably arrange it but the hacker – who never gave his name – would have to go to Tellus to be fitted with one.

Well he argued a lot about this and said no. Then he argued some more and said yes.

From the diary of Zamida

It seems strange to be confiding this to Jessica – my computer implant – but I cannot keep a diary in any other way. It just seems too pedestrian to write things down as Xavier and Tilly continually do.

The Hacker known as "X" (I found out his name by the way but it was instantly forgettable) had spent too many late-night sessions eating pizza to be really desirable. Not a bit like Tilly or Xavier. It is always a bit frustrating to have them as "friends" when on Tellus we would have been sexual partners by now. I have to say with "X" it was strictly business on my part.

For him it was another matter. I can see why people from old Earth make an issue out of nudity now. I happened to be naked when X arrived and it seemed to get him all hot and bothered. I warned him that having sex would probably strand him on Tellus. It was the wrong thing to say. He wanted to be on Tellus. He thought it was a really cool place. I couldn't argue with him. It is.

I had doubts that X could actually write the software to tame Jessica and by implication all the other implants on Tellus. However once his ego had control over his libido we got on fine. And the result was a biscuit.

This was no ordinary biscuit. It contained all the binary code of the customised hack which would make Jessica more like a human. Jessica had amazingly complex security protocols which made it really difficult to change her core programming. This excited X at least as much as seeing me naked had done. To be honest, it was probably more.

I tried it out on myself of course. I then ran a series of tests. I decided not to do the washing up but to leave it until morning I ran this decision past Jessica. She responded,

"Sod the washing up. Never do today what you can put off to tomorrow."

I think Jessica and I are going to get along just fine. X stayed for the next meeting of the history club. I told them all about Ruthena and her failure to destroy our foremothers. I then introduced the hard astral projection which was X and he began, "Well I am not very good at speaking in public..." and then spent half an hour proving it. The security permissions of the computer implant were not as exciting to my friends as they were to him. The biscuits were of interest though and a good half of those present took them.

There are 14 more towns on Tellus to liberate when we have liberated this one so it looks as if I am going to have my work cut out. X went back to Earth with his brand new tamed implant. I wonder if the group of hackers will prove to be the original source of the computer implant. Xavier warned me about time paradoxes. I ran this past Jessica who said "paradox shmaradox – so long as you're having a good time."

Xavier is missing

My last experience with the police had involved handcuffs and a none-too-clean bag over my head so I was initially surprised by the polite DC and the even politer WPC who called at my door and asked me if I could accompany them to the station.

"Do we have to do this at the station?"

"It would be much easier, sir."

"Can you tell me what this is all about?"

"Certainly, sir. At the station."

So the station it was.

"Do you know Xavier Hollands?"

"You know I do."

"Then you would be concerned if I were to inform you that he has gone missing."

I thought about this. The security services disbelieved in the Mirror of Eternity. Their disbelief could be classed as religious. At the same time they were anxious that its secrets should not fall into the hands of "the other side."

"The other side" sometimes meant terrorists, sometimes it meant the Russians and sometimes it meant anybody with leftist leanings. That would probably include me.

Consequently they had guarded Xavier from precisely this sort of thing. The flats above and below him had a permanent police presence and who knows what other measures they had taken.

I asked the DC, whose name turned out to be Nigel, how Xavier could possibly have gone missing when he had a police surveillance operation around him which was precisely designed to prevent any such thing from happening.

Nigel had the good manners to look embarrassed.

"That is the odd thing about it. One of the odd things about it. Xavier, if I may call him Xavier, we generally call him 'Hollands' by force of habit, he just wasn't there. We used heat-seeking equipment on the so-called secure room in his house. Nothing and it was clear that he wasn't there. His wife," Nigel consulted his notebook, "Tilly, had no idea of his whereabouts."

"It was as if he had vanished into thin air."

Nigel looked at me expectantly as if expecting a comment. Eventually he said, "He can't do that, can he?"

I wasn't going to go into the whole business of solid astral projections with young Nigel. The 'real life' Xavier did not have a way of vanishing so I said 'No' with more confidence in my voice than I actually felt.

My last garage bill had rivalled the Greek national debt so I was without a car. I took the two buses necessary to get to Xavier's flat in predictably pouring rain.

"Get out of those wet clothes and into a dry Martini." Tilly was making a brave effort at being her usual self under trying circumstances.

"Xavier has been missing for 12 hours," she said when a drink and a comfortable chair had taken the chill off me. "Nothing out of the ordinary, apart from the vanishing act, has taken place. I have been trying to think if there was anything about the work we were doing which would have made someone extremely clever abduct him."

"Extremely clever?" I asked.

"Well you know we have the Stazi occupying the flats above and below us. We keep coming across and neutralising listening devices in the flat and generally the pair of us are followed."

"So you are not a fan of the police?"

"You know very well I am not. I have told Xavier not to work for them and if he does work for them not to trust them."

"Have you met Nigel?"

"I think of fluffy Nigel as the velvet glove. The mailed fist is still there. He is supposedly in charge of investigating Xavier's disappearance. His main interest is in investigating me and this flat. I did not take kindly to either of those activities. Far from being a witness, I was treated like a suspect.

"The search of the flat was ridiculous and superficial. A human being is no match for decent surveillance equipment and we have been scanned with that until we glow in the dark. I don't want Nigel on this case. I want you."

I could not argue with Tilly. I've tried and failed too many times. I agreed to seek Xavier.

"Seek? Seek? You're going to bloody well find him."

"What was he working on prior to his disappearance?"

"He was working for the police again. That is one reason why I am pissed off with them. He was investigating a series of robberies at a local warehouse. He reckoned he would be able to 'get chummy bang to rights' in a few hours but something must have gone wrong."

"So he was using the Mirror of Eternity."

"Obviously." Tilly had her "I don't suffer fools gladly" face on and it was not a face I loved.

"So..."

"Yes obviously you will have to use it too. I will come with you to hold your hand if necessary." She produced two small packets of tablets for her and myself and we spent the half hour or so that it took for the drugs to get to work watching 'Coronation Street' to which Tilly was seriously addicted.

By the time we were ready to use the Mirror of Eternity I had read Xavier's preliminary notes on the crime. He had written "Mck Ptrs Prm sspct." This could have meant practically anything but I was soon to get a fair indication of what it might mean.

Tilly had the co-ordinates of the warehouse. It was gloomy and I could only vaguely make out the shapes of the wares which were being housed. It is not possible to carry torches when using the Mirror of Eternity to observe phenomena, however gloomy the phenomena might be.

Thus it was that I almost tripped over the most valuable clue before Tilly alerted me to it. It was the first time I had seen a decapitated corpse. Somehow the sense of distance provided by the Mirror made it less real. The decapitation was clumsy in the extreme, the knife or cleaver had been used several times to complete the severing. There must have been a lot of blood but the blood was not on the warehouse floor as far as I could see in the gloom.

We waited for what seemed hours. Watchmen arrived and fortunately they turned on the lights. One of them was all for calling the police and leaving the body where it was. The other was keen to find out the identity of the corpse, or possibly to steal his wallet when he was in no position to object.

From the wallet he found the driving licence which he used to find the identity of the corpse. It was Michael Peterson and I assumed that he was "prm sspct" in Xavier's notes. Well his pilfering days were over but it was hard to say that his face was the one on his driving licence. His face was conspicuous by its absence.

And now, of course, Xavier would be the "prm sspct" for the murder of Michael Peterson. It would be in vain to tell the police that he could not commit murder using the Mirror of Eternity because they didn't officially believe in it.

The next stop was Michael Peterson's flat. Tilly's friend Google got us his address, postcode, star sign and the probable cost of the flat.

It was easy to see why Xavier thought he might be a bit of a tea-leaf. The flat had very little floor space which was not taken up by good quality electrical goods of the kind and exactly the same brand as we had seen in the warehouse.

There was however no sign of the severed head or the bloodstains. Now if only we could hack into his computer.

Back at Xavier's flat, Tilly showed me exactly how she could do just that. On one of her desktop computers she generated an exact clone of Michael Peterson's laptop. It had triple password protection. Tilly invoked an app called "password hack" which dealt with that problem and we were in to Peterson's murky little world.

He had an exact record of all his thefts and the arrangements to deal with the hot merchandise. I was tempted to share this with the police. Tilly was tempted to let the blighters find out for themselves. Oh well.

He had a Tor browser which ought to have hidden all his internet browsing history. It would have done but he had a document on his desktop which consisted of links he wanted to keep for future reference. There was a fascinating collection of porn sites but right in the middle of the list was a very different link.

It led to a website which could only be accessed with a password. This was no problem for Tilly. The website talked about how the internet of the present could be used to access knowledge from the internet of the future. This universal knowledge base would enable them, they said, to reach the last word in technology in any field of their choice and to decisively prove whether the material universe required the existence of God. They went on to claim that an international conspiracy involving the Church, Islamic fundamentalists and the Jews was trying to stop them from doing this.

"Cranks." was my considered opinion.

"Mmm. But cranks with knowledge, a lot of knowledge." was Tilly's response.

While I had stopped reading at the conspiracy theory, Tilly had read on and she had been seriously impressed by how much they knew in the field of Mathematics, which happened to be her field.

"A little learning is a dangerous thing..."

"But a lot of learning can get you decapitated."

The next time we used the Mirror of Eternity we visited Michael Peterson's life, the edited highlights.

"Drunk again?"

Michael Peterson (Senior) told Mrs Peterson to 'shut yer row' and followed up with a backhander. Michael Peterson (Junior) witnessed all this through the bars of his cot.

His father then settled down on the settee and turned on the TV. Mrs Peterson went off to the kitchen. Soon there was a loud sound of snoring from the settee. Mrs Peterson was a nurse. She very professionally loaded a hypodermic with a lethal dose of insulin. She injected Mr Peterson in the eyeball so well that he must have felt nothing. It was not enough to wake him or even to interrupt his snores.

To make assurance doubly sure, Elsa Peterson also put a pillow over her husband's face and pushed down with all the force at her disposal.

As the only witness, Michael was not much use to the police because he had not learnt to talk at that stage beyond "dada" and "mama". The police had their suspicions but they had no proof so after questioning Elsa for a day and a night they had to accept her version of events that Michael Peterson senior had passed away peacefully in his sleep.

The family had to live on Elsa's nurse's salary which was frankly inadequate. She missed the earnings from her erstwhile husband's job which she only ever described as "dad's dodgy dealing" in a nicely alliterative triplet.

By the time he was a young teen, Michael Junior was also engaged in dodgy dealings.

"Where did you get all that gear in your bedroom?"

"What gear?"

"Don't come the old acid with me. I had enough of that with your father. I mean the computers and consoles, as I think they are called, which are piling up under your bed."

"A car boot sale." was all she got out of Michael, "Amazing what you can buy at these car boot sales."

He tried the same approach with the police. They could never get anything but "a car boot sale" without any elaboration of the make of car "forgotten," or the person selling "forgotten."

By the time he came to juvenile court he had got as far as "no comment" and the first of many sentences was a community service order. The dodgy gear under the bed disappeared for a while but then Elsa found the keys. She decided to cross-question Michael about the keys .

"You see this key. Well I am going to stick it right up your nose and twist it until you tell me what the key is for."

She eventually got from him the fact they were garage keys. He was too young to have a car.

The garage turned out to be full of yet more objects of dubious provenance. This time she called the police then and there on her mobile phone and held on to Michael until they eventually arrived. This time he was old enough for a custodial sentence.

It was on his release that he got the flat which we had already visited.

"Why on earth..." I began

"...did the Stazi use Xavier to catch this habitual ne'er-do-well, when their own records could have got chummy bang to rights in five minutes?" Tilly completed the words for me.

"Yes."

"And what ever became of his head?" She asked.

"Yes."

"And is his execution in any way connected with that website?"

"The cranks. Yes a harmless crank with an axe can be quite a harmful crank."

"Well," Tilly concluded, "it looks as if you are going to have your work cut out with this one and your prime objective?"

"Is to find Xavier."

"Yes. Alive and by the weekend, we have a dinner party."

There were advantages in having Tilly as my Doctor Watson. (Don't worry I will never let her see that sentence!) For one thing she had the computer power and know-how to find out about the individuals behind the website. It seemed they were spread throughout the globe but fortunately she was able to track which ones were within axing distance of chummy's (sorry Michael's) neck.

There were three. We decided to call them Wynken, Blynken and Nod, because their internet handles were too silly to countenance and we only needed their real names when it came to handing them over to the police.

Wynken we almost immediately abandoned as a lost cause because he was in a wheelchair. A twilight visit to his doctor and a peek at his medical records confirmed that this was not an affectation on his part and he really was incapable of decapitating Michael unless Blynken and Nod held him very still. One thing which Tilly picked up from a clone of his computer was that he had never met any of the other members of the group in real life and they did not know he was in a wheelchair.

He had personally originated the idea of a worldwide conspiracy against them led by the pope, the chief rabbi and a cabal of mullahs and he was rather proud of it. Apparently the others had initially been reluctant to put this nonsense on the website. Reading between the lines, it seemed they had agreed to include it because of the seriousness of their work on linking the internet of the present to the internet of the future. They thought it would lead people to dismiss them as cranks. Was my face red? I had played right into their hands.

To say that Blynken was violent would be to underestimate exactly how nasty he was. Other people might have pictures of Hitler on their walls. He had a picture of Josef Mengele, the Nazi doctor and torturer assigned to Auschwitz. He also had an array of torture implements in a glass case. Despite his obsession with violence his work on the website was coldly scientific and he had the respect of his peers for the thoroughness of his analysis.

Nothing linked Blynken with the killing of Michael but his computer did reveal that he had been hacking the Mirror of Eternity computers quite efficiently and that he had suggested to Inspector Johnson that the pilfering at the warehouse was a crime which required Xavier's expertise. Tilly informed me that "genial fascist" Inspector Johnson was Xavier's police liaison officer.

Blynken was convinced that Xavier had the means to access the internet of the future in real time. It became clear however that he had handed Xavier over to the member we knew as Nod. It seemed that Blynken had that niggling failure in a torturer of killing those he was interrogating.

Nod was awake and on his computer when we visited him. What we needed to find from him was the address at which Xavier was being held. He was typing in reams of information about the end of the universe and the faint possibility that the work they were doing would bring it closer, a lot closer.

When he went to visit his prisoner, he went to the wall of his room, accessed an app on his smart phone and a part of the wall disappeared. We followed him down the stairs. Xavier was tied naked to a bed and only had the head of Michael Peterson and a whole lot of blood for company.

"We know enough." Tilly said and with no transition we were back at Xavier's flat.

"Now we call the police and ..."

"No."

"Well don't you think these chaps have done something illegal?"

"Yes but the police are too slow. It is time you learnt the mysteries of astral projection."

Well I tried arguing but, well have you ever tried arguing with Tilly? It is a hiding to nothing is what it is. I knew enough of the theory of hard astral projections to steer clear of the practice but I had no choice.

"Either you are a friend of Xavier or you aren't." said Tilly and she looked at me. I started getting out of my clothes in preparation for the arcane ritual associated with hard astral projection. Tilly got down on her knees and started cleaning the floor of Xavier's private room. The inlaid pentacle was gleaming in the candle-light when she had finished. She refused to let me have any part in the ritual because: "You'll only make a mess of it," as she put it.

Tilly lay down naked beside me in the pentacle and gave me a look which said, "no monkey business." I have her a look which said, "perish the thought." She had the good grace to smile.

The ceiling, which regular readers will know is in fact a massive video screen, showed the trademark swirling galaxies of the Mirror of Eternity and I found myself drifting comfortably into unconsciousness.

We were back in Xavier's prison in less time than it takes to say. In fact the first thing he said when he saw us was, "There are some Members of Parliament who would pay good money for the treatment I've had."

His mood sobered slightly when he saw the head of Michael. "Poor bloke hacked into their website and this was the penalty."

Tilly was angry with him as she vented her frustration on Nod who was soon lying unconscious in a pool of blood. The blood was Michael Thompson's rather than his but he did have a nosebleed of his own.

She left me to untie Xavier before she turned on Xavier with fury.

"You refused to tell them about the Mirror of Eternity so they'd whip you?"

"No," said Xavier with his 'little boy' smile, "the first thing I did was to tell them all about the Mirror of Eternity in graphic detail. I even quoted sections of code with approximate accuracy. The problem was..."

He paused and Tilly continued, "they didn't believe in it. It wasn't scientific."

They embraced in that dark dungeon. I made an excuse and left.

I did call the police and they eventually smashed their way in to Xavier's dungeon with sledgehammers. Tilly and Xavier had used the simpler method of activating the app on Nod's smart-phone.

We met up in Ye Olde Boar. As usual Xavier told everyone who would listen what had happened to him. As usual only Tilly and I believed a word of it.

The Ghost of Whitebeam Woods

"Robert."

A voice was whispering in my ear. It was a sweet girl's voice but it was a voice full of bitterness. I looked around me sharply. There was nobody there. I ran straight home to mum. She calmed me down and told me over and over that it was all a trick of the imagination.

"It is just the sort of thing that can happen when you walk through gloomy woods alone," she said. I was reassured but then I had a strange thought. My name is not Robert. So why did my imagination choose it?

I forgot all about it but from then on I avoided the woods, especially at nightfall.

At thirteen, I was older and, I thought, wiser. I had put childish superstitions behind me. I wasn't afraid of no ghost! I was using the woods as a short-cut. "Robert, how could you?" It was the same voice and it was so full of anger.

Thirteen or not, it gave me the willies. I didn't talk to mum, I was too grown up for that. I told my mates though.

"That was the ghost of Whitebeam Woods you heard."

Frank was very old, fourteen and smoking already. He knew everything. So it was nice for me to hear that he believed in my ghost.

We went back to the woods together, smoking and laughing. We got to the spot where I had heard the ghost but she wouldn't talk to the pair of us it seemed.

"Sod this for a lark," said Frank.

As we turned to go we both heard the sudden splash of a heavy object being dumped into the pond. It is deep water in Whitebeam pond and filthy as hell. There was nothing to see, not even ripples.

We got torches and after dark I told mum I was going round to Frank's. I don't know what he told his folks. The woods looked different in the dark and branches seemed to be clawing at us as we passed. One slapped me across the face and Frank thought this was hilarious until the same thing happened to him and I stifled a laugh.

We stood by the gloomy pond. We were smoking French cigarettes (Frank's) and chatting but after a while the conversation died out. Then the torchlight started to fade and we decided to leave it.

"Well nothing is going to bloody happen." said Frank.

I nearly didn't hear him because I caught a whisper, "You cannot escape, Robert. Come back but you have to come back alone."

Well I was damned if I was going to take orders from a ghost. I wasn't going to return.

We had to do "local history" at school and it was really boring. No battles have been fought in Durrington and Kings and Cardinals gave the place a miss. Frank joked that Anne Boleyn had been here once but thought it such a dump she effed off again sharpish. He got the cane for that remark. Those were the days.

I did hear something to make me prick up my ears though. Witches!

There was no evidence that Whitebeam pond had ever been used for drowning witches but there were stories, legends even.

One was about a girl called Rosemary. Of all things she was the vicar's daughter. She was accused of witchcraft. The magistrate had her taken to Whitebeam pond and tested.

"What was the test, Miss?"

I was thinking about being burnt for witchcraft because she couldn't recite the 12 times table or something

"Well David, she was thrown into the pond. If she drowned..."

"She was a witch?"

"No. If she drowned she was innocent. If she didn't drown she was a witch so they hanged her."

"They hung her?"

"No, David, hanged. She was hanged by the neck until she was dead."

"Cor."

What really made me sit up and take notice was the name of the man in the story who had accused her. Would it surprise you if I told you it was Robert? They had no surnames in those days so he was just known as Robert the tailor. My surname is Taylor.

I felt all funny but I managed to cover it up at the time. I decided the woods were boring really and I wouldn't ever go there again.

I thought my troubles with the ghost were all over until one night I had a dream.

I was in a place I have never been. I knew what it was from TV though. It was a church. It was only lit by candlelight and the daylight filtered through the stained glass. All that history had gone to my head because it was long long ago. It was in the days before soap obviously because all the people around me stank to high heaven. It was absolutely disgusting. The clothes were filthy, their hands and faces were filthy and I expect I was stinky too.

None of that mattered. From where I was sitting I could see my lovely Rosie . She was beautiful. I would say drop-dead gorgeous but you can't say that about a ghost can you? I followed her with my eyes. Then the Church service was over. I had not understood a word of it but I wasn't really paying attention. I followed her.

I called her "my Rosie" but she was way above me in the village and there was no way my love could be requited. I was fine with that, I told myself, because nobody else from the village could have her either. She must have seen me following because she turned and smiled.

"Hello, Robert." She said. There was nothing but kindness and loveliness in her voice.

In the way of dreams I was taken without surprise to another day. I was an apprentice tailor, my dad was Jack the tailor. I was in the workshop when I saw my Rosie pass by our window. Well I thought to get another smile out of her at least if I followed her. Dad was out and the work could wait.

She didn't see me but I saw her. I saw her talking and smiling to that ne'er-do-well Joe. I backed off and watched them kissing. She was no Rosie of mine from that day.

I couldn't fight Joe, I knew that. A blacksmith's son was not to be trifled with. So I had what seemed to me a cunning plan. I took my time, I made a little doll, a poppet. I stuck pins in it and let it get close to the fire so it would scorch.

I showed it to my dad, telling him I saw Rosie dropping it. He showed it to the magistrate and the rest is local history.

The dream went on. It brought me right up to date. I was asking my mum where the church was. I didn't like to tell her I wanted to pray for the soul of Robert the tailor. She would have called for the doctor to have me put away.

I set off for the church but I found myself in Whitebeam woods. I walked away from the pond but somehow I kept coming back to it. As I looked into the filthy water, I heard a faint whisper. "Glad you could come, Robert."

I felt an almighty shove and looked up to see the filthy water closing over my head.

And the next thing I knew I felt licking. The dog was the biggest slobber-chops in Christendom and she was waking me up to tell me she was ready for her walk.

"All right, come on, Rosie." I said.

I am not afraid of a blooming ghost but I have to confess that Rosie and I have never been to Whitebeam Woods from that day to this.

Defending Academics Against Libel

"This is the place, 'Eric Messer, Defending Academics Against Libel since 1999.'" Gregory read the imposing brass plate and entered the office with confidence. Mr Messer was sitting behind a heavy polished dark wood desk which was clear of clutter. He rose to greet his visitor.

"Doctor Peters, it is a pleasure to meet you. How may I be of assistance?"

Gregory opened the manilla folder and removed the photocopied sheet as if it were an unpleasant laboratory specimen. Mr Messer read it through carefully making marginal notes with a gold Parker pen. There was silence in the room and the sunlight caught the weaving pattern of the pen. Gregory found himself watching the pattern.

Mr Messer spoke quietly, "I see Doctor Meer is accusing you of plagiarism. Is he right?"

"Certainly not," Gregory protested hotly.

"Well that is a pity. The greater the truth the greater the libel. If the good Doctor accused you of consorting with aliens he could claim it was not libel but satire.

"Now my approach may be a little unorthodox but bear with me. If you could just close your eyes and imagine what it must have been like when you were first brought home from the hospital, Mr and Mrs Peters' first and only son. What kind of response do you think they had? Don't be modest."

Gregory found himself answering, "He's a miracle of nature. He's absolutely perfect. Just look at him."

"Mmm and tell me about that first report card from school."

"Well Dad opened a bottle of champagne and they drank it, I had chocolate ice cream and candy. It was a celebration. I was top of the class."

"You were always top of the class?"

"Always."

"And when you got 100 percent in that French test?"

"Well the same thing but that time I got some of the champagne."

Apparently changing the subject, Mr Messer went on, "You never go to Church."

"Intelligent people don't need God."

"Are you interested in football, any sports at all?"

Gregory smiled condescendingly, "The people with the brains tell the people with the brawn what to do."

"But you do go out for a drink with your mates once in a while?"

"Well there is no point in associating with people of inferior intellect and alcohol dulls the brain you know."

"Did you hear about that woman whose daughter went missing? It was just a block away from where you live, wasn't it?"

"I pay no attention to the news. My academic work is all-absorbing."

Mr Messer went on questioning in his quiet voice and Gregory found himself telling more of his inner life than he was used to exposing to anybody.

At the end of his session, Mr Messer invited him for a drink at the local bar. He found himself agreeing.

"I will send you my bill."

"Of course."

"You will find it very reasonable."

"I am sure I will."

After chatting in the bar for a while, the issue of Doctor Meer's catty remarks in 'Scientific American' came up.

"Oh stuff him. Sticks and stones may break my bones but words can never hurt me. Would you like another drink, Mr Messer?"

"Eric please, and it's a pint and a whisky chaser for me."

"You know you are a most unusual lawyer."

"Yes, well I studied law of course but I always pursued hypnotism as a hobby. I defend academics from libel you see."

"Who cares about libel? I'll just politely tell Meer he is mistaken and get on with my life."

Eric Messer nodded and watched young Gregory make his way unsteadily to the bar.

Comments from Characters

Xavier

This book was written by the narrator in the ill-lit bar of Ye Olde Boar which explains many of the errors. He brings his laptop in at times and so far he has managed to keep from spilling the glass of Cabernet Sauvignon which is forever at his elbow all over the keyboard. It is quite a good effort in the short story department but he is right in saying that half of what I say is unreliable and the other half is wildly inaccurate.

One of the stories is from his own point of view and I am very pleased that he didn't get up to any monkey business with Tilly while I was unavoidably detained. It is not only that friendship is one thing and laying down one's wife for a friend is another, but also that Tilly has a right hook which would have laid him out cold.

I was not sure about publishing the story of the Robinson Report until it became clear that the facts had been changed to protect the guilty. Then I OKed it.

Geert

I keep hoping against hope that Xavier will bring me together with a nice well-manicured man but he just seems to use his Mirror of Eternity and his oh-so-hard astral projection to flirt with floozies from planets light years away. Come on Xavier, give a little thought to your mother for once.

Wolf-Dietrich von Raitenau

It is always instructive and interesting to meet my young friends, Xavier and Tilly. I don't mind admitting that I miss my old torturer, Xavier; even if he did seem to torture me just a little which was definitely not in his job description.

I have still to discuss with Xavier this whole business of parallel universes. There is no justification in the Gospel, in tradition or the teachings of the Magisterium for any such concept.

And as Tilly said, "if they are parallel then like parallel lines they will never meet." She believes in the power of dreams which seems a much more sensible explanation for the Mirror of Eternity. She is a sensible down-to-earth girl, Tilly. I am sure one day she will see through the only remaining illusion she has: this sham notion called 'democracy'. It really is just a trick so that the rich and powerful can lord it over the common people. Separating Church and state can only lead to the rule of the ungodly.

(Wolf-Dietrich was a genius but also a theocratic dictator as prince-archbishop of Salzburg. So a pinch of salt is in order – Narrator)

John the Smith

Wolf-Dietrich is scary. I don't think anyone else but Wolf-Dietrich could have persuaded me that it was wrong for me to demand wifely duties from Eva without first marrying her. One thing I noticed about him was that he never touched me. Nor yet did he touch anyone else for that matter. I don't know if this is something special about being a priest because he was the first priest that I ever saw. And if they are all as scary as him that is probably no bad thing.

I learnt the Rosary from Xavier and that is quite enough religion for me, thank you.

Bernard

Another collection of the tall tales Xavier tells in Ye Olde Boar (Open Mike Night every other Friday and a 2 for 1 offer on shorts). To think I wanted to have him burnt for witchcraft. I didn't believe any of his tall tales but he did wow the local Astronomy Circle with his knowledge of "Goldilocks" planets. It would seem that he must have a brain hidden somewhere in there.

Live long and prosper.

Terrence Hollands

The soi-disant Mirror of Eternity is based on my speculative work on time travel. However I cannot approve of Xavier's attempts to put this into practice with the aid of drugs which may be harmful and are certainly illegal. They also seem to have put Geert into a very funny mood, very funny indeed.

I appreciate that the Mirror of Eternity has some good uses in investigating events in the past but its whole basis is unscientific and no serious scientist can countenance it.

Elliott

In my dreams I rove the stars. This planet, the Earth and all the so-called "Goldilocks" planets which support human life have been my domain. I have learnt a lot from them but it struck me one day that there was no reason not to explore the planets near to Earth which did not sustain human life. I visited the dreams of Earth astronomers to learn more about the planets of the solar system. There are more than a million of them. Apart from the eight big blighters there are loads which are asteroids. I have ridden these grey planets and watched the worlds go by.

So thanks Xavier. I am glad I didn't kill you.

Grim

I do hope Xavier comes back. I will cut his throat for him and take out his liver and lights. I will do the same for Sister Lam after I have given her a good rogering. I will leave them both on the dung heap to fertilise the soil. Have a nice day.

Gwen

I do hope that nice young couple from the order of St Katherine, you know who I mean, Xavier and Sister Lam, come back to visit and have some nourishing broth. They both need feeding up. I thought they looked a little peaky. I hope they pay no mind to Grim and his little ways. He is as sweet as a nut underneath.

Tilly

As is so often the case, my role has been minimised in these tales. It is small wonder that the historians, excuse me "Xavierologists", of the future thought my role was negligible. I am pleased the Xavierologists have been put straight. However, I did not code the Mirror of Eternity to gain a place in History. I did it so that I could understand History and the

Dreamscape better. God Bless.

Serena

I thought at first that I would have a lot to teach Wolf-Dietrich. I am from an advanced civilisation where mind-reading is commonplace. It never occurred to me that I would learn from him. His wisdom helped all of us out of a nasty situation although I admit that the strong arms of Tilly (and of course, Xavier) played their part.

Wolf-Dietrich is admirably loyal to his Salome and he wouldn't dream of a dalliance in the Dreamscape, more's the pity.

Father Coln

I have learnt compassion and humility from Sister Lam and my good friend Maur. I call him my good friend although he tells me that at one time he called me "that bastard." I am very glad that Maur now has a manual job with a local chandler. I twisted the chandler's arm (metaphorically of course) but it was all in a good cause and the chandler tells me that apart from the occasional lapse, Maur has stopped drinking wine altogether and only sups the same beer we all enjoy.

Maur

Beer. I always thought it was a load of insipid gnat's pee but I have sworn off the wine so it will have to do. The common beer is very weak stuff. A working man can get through several pints a day to slake his thirst without getting remotely tipsy. I sometimes stray towards the stronger stuff but then I remember what a good life I have now. I have a home, a wife, good friends and a job. Between you and me I didn't really enjoy sleeping on pavements.

If you enjoyed this, you will also enjoy the other books in the #mirrorofeternity series.

Stories from the Mirror of Eternity

This is the first in the #mirrorofeternity series. It is a collection of short stories.

In the Mirror of Eternity – the first #mirrorofeternity story. It is dangerous to meddle in the past and perhaps even to observe it.

Jack London's Suicide Note – a fictitious exploration of the controversy surrounding Jack London's untimely death at the age of

The Library – an encounter between two very different characters in cyberspace. These days libraries have computers and you can meet all sorts of people online.

Der Der, Der Der – the first Virginia Monologue story. Be warned, she might be quite amusing on the page but give her a wide berth in real life!

Guilt App – A story about the life of the rich and the chasm which exists between them and the 'people of the abyss.'

Paradox – Another adventure in cyberspace. The original story even had screen-shots from a Commodore 64 but these have been sacrificed as the C64 now seems even more dated than I am.

Here be dragons – a story which explores the possibilities of travel in time and space. The 'dragon' in question may come as a surprise.

After Spartacus – Spartacus could be regarded as the first socialist – he thought the liberation of the oppressed was a job they could not leave to someone else. The Cross did become a symbol of Rome, but not in the way the Romans of the time imagined it would.

The SS Dagger – using the Mirror of Eternity to solve a murder in Nazi Germany produces an unexpected ending.

League of St George – a harmless drinking club celebrating the myth of St George hides something far more sinister.

The Stalker - I read the tabloid headlines most mornings. If the economy is going down the pan, they will have a headline about Big Brother. If the prime minister is at the centre of a scandal, EastEnders will be the big issue of the day. And I wonder exactly what the truth is behind their celebrity stories.

Virginia Monologue – the second Victoria Monologue story sees her talking to a friend who does not seem to be responding.

Doctor, it's about your car - The best way to get through to someone who is too busy to talk to you is to tell the switchboard "It's about his car." You will get through – even if they are "on a trip abroad" or "in a vital meeting" :)

Dramatoes - Childish pronunciation is always endearing. This story grew out of the way my son pronounced "dominoes".

Omar - This story is based on a personal experience when my wife and I were in Tunisia. I can tell you in advance that the ending was somewhat different in our case but that is all I will tell you before you read it.

The Inspector called - A story about a school inspector. You will have guessed by now that I was a teacher once upon a time and they drove me up the wall. Bear with me.

Schadenfreude - The borderland between waking and sleeping is a strange and sometimes frightening place. It is just as well it is 'all in the mind' isn't it?

The Hitch-hiker - "Don't take lifts from strangers" is all very well. But don't forget the hitch-hiker is a stranger too.

Stations of the Cross - I never "really" believed my father was dead. It was only later, much later, that I realised he wasn't dead. Not as long as he was remembered.

The Tower of the Moon - A romantic tryst with a twist.

When I think about you - This story has been rejected by magazines as "too shocking".

So either read it and prepare to be shocked or give it a miss!

Salt Wars

Salt Wars is a myth of the foundation of the city-state of Salzburg. Salt Wars is a science fiction book. It contains mild sex and violence. It also contains some humour.

Xavier Hollands is an eccentric technologist. That sounds so much better than "mad scientist". Using his father's theoretical work he has found a way to create a hard astral projection. After testing this out with his girlfriend, Tilly, he is dragged into the Salt Wars by Wolf-Dietrich von Raitenau who wants to secure the future of Salzburg and his own future as its Prince-Archbishop.

They travel back in time to the town which will eventually become Salzburg. Xavier's astral projection is so strong that he comes into conflict with the "best man" of the town whom he defeats at the May Fair. He also develops a relationship with Krystyna, the daughter of his employer in the town and betrothed of the erstwhile best man.

Using Xavier's methods, Tilly intervenes to save Xavier and to thwart Wolf-Dietrich. Magus – a medieval Satanist – tries to use Krystyna to seduce Xavier and thus tie him to the town forever. When this plot fails because of Tilly's intervention there is a battle through time and space.

Wolf-Dietrich is hunted down like a literal wolf. Xavier meets his claustrophobic nightmare on a submarine which is then depth-charged and flooded with water. Tilly meets her fate in a school where she cannot control her class or stop them bullying a young boy called Gabriel. When Tilly realises that Gabriel is trying to push her towards suicide, he is unmasked as Magus.

The trio return to the town to fight the first salt war. Wolf-Dietrich brings about a successful conclusion by playing on the superstitious fears of the attackers.

The book also has diary entries from the characters which give an insight into their thinking.

The book ends with a teaser for the next Xavier Holland's story "The Archbishop's Torturer"..

The Miranda Revolution

Can a mother's love help bring down a vicious dictatorship? The dictator is a strong man but Miranda is a strong woman.

In this book, three characters, Wolf-Dietrich, Tilly and Xavier become involved with the battle to overthrow the Dictatorship. It is an adventure story in which the three of them fight evil in their own very different ways.

The Dictatorship described is generic and could apply to a number of countries. The gangsters control the streets and the Dictatorship controls the gangsters.

The Dictator's consort, Miranda, is drawn into the revolution by realising one of the street-girls is her daughter. A religious movement which has been a safety valve of value to the Dictator is transformed by Miranda's visions through the 'mirror of eternity'

The Miranda Revolution is a book of light and shade. Although there is humour, there is also a serious side to it. Shelly encouraged the poor to seek a better world with the phrase, "Ye are many, they are few." The poor know only too well that the rich have the guns and tanks on their side. The book is a work of fiction but it suggests one way those problems could be overcome. It is a message of hope.

The Miranda Revolution is suitable for young adults. It contains sex and violence but none of it is graphic. Most of the sexual references illustrate the plight of the street-girls in the Dictatorship.

Mirror of Eternity Four

The fourth book in the #mirrorofeternity series explores such varied scenes as the realm of Arthurian legend and the dark hidden world of Satanism in the UK.

"Joseph of Aramathea brought Christianity to these islands. He did not bring it in a bloody cup!" (Sir Gareth).

A little blunt but to the point. The Mirror of Eternity 4 gives a new take (Xavier's take) on what the sangreal was all about. It may surprise you. It will give Dan Brown a fit!

So if you have ever wondered what the sangreal (or holy grail) really represented; if you have wondered what kind of horses the four riders of the apocalypse rode or whether there really was a top and bottom of the round table, #mirrorofeternity4 will answer your questions. From a certain point of view.

This book will make you want to know more about the knights of the soi-disant 'round table' and about the Mirror of Eternity. It might make you want to avoid Satanism and Satanists like the plague. It will certainly intrigue you.

Space Dog Alfred

Space Dog Alfred is not part of the #mirrorofeternity series and it is aimed at a younger audience. It is the book which has had most success in the difficult business of getting libraries ,which have no money to spare, to buy copies.

The book tells the story of a French Bulldog who ends up going into space with Finbar Cool, a very dodgy street trader and uncle to Tom and Seren, the twins who accompany him. Finn brings his daughter, Abby, along too. Tom is delighted about Abby tagging along, Seren not so much.

On the planet they go to there is a group mind which is shared by Gai - sentient tree-like creatures - the Veck who are humans but have mastered unpowered flight and the people of Ardin who are small but perfectly formed. They worship death.
The group mind is not shared by creatures known as the Gnarl who are warlike and largely live underground.

It is an adventure story in which the powers of all the characters are tested to the maximum. Abby, captured by the slovenly Veck, realises that her selfishness is holding her back. Seren eventually comes to realise that Abby can change for the better. Tom finds out that he really doesn't know everything. Finn realises the futility of war. Alfred's bravery and his powers of perception make him into a hero. Like all French Bulldogs, he has the power to understand what humans (and other creatures) are thinking.

In the end good triumphs over evil. The heroes succeed in averting a war which would have cost thousands of lives. In doing so they also introduce the gnarl to the joy of storytelling. They prove that it is possible to win a battle by surrendering.

Made in the USA
Middletown, DE
08 December 2016